HOLIDAYS
WITH
SUNDAE

Conversations with My Cat ~ *me too*
"5"

James T. Baker

Second Printing, 2004

ISBN: 0-9661317-0-3

Green Hills Press
P. O. Box 394
Brookings, SD 57006

**To the Girl of my Autumn
who walks in silence toward
the Setting Sun**

CHRISTMAS

"**W**hy?"

I have to tell you I was stunned when Sundae said "Why" to me that day because I didn't know she could talk. I knew she could think, I knew she could reason, I knew she could reflect because I had watched her do it. I had seen the results. She almost always got things right. I knew she was smart, that part was never in doubt. She and I had lived together for over six months, and I had come to accept the fact that she and I were on just about the same intellectual level. But that she could talk, well, it had just never occured to me. Sundae is my cat.

"What?" I said to her, trying to hold the car on the road while I glanced with shock down at her face looking at me through the bars of her cage, which sat on the floor, while I tried to process this thing my ears told me was true but my brain refused to register.

"What yourself," she said back to me through the bars. Her eyes accused me of every kind of evil for keeping her in her pen. I had placed the cage on the floor facing me because I had been told that a cat should be able to see her master on a trip but should not be able to see the road. I was told that seeing the rapid movement of cars and trees would just confuse and frighten her, but that seeing me would reassure her.

"What did you. . . Did you say Why?" I stammered.

"Yes, as a matter of fact, I did."

"I. . .didn't know you could talk."

"Well, now you do."

"How. . .long. . .?

"How long have I been able to talk?" she said. "I don't know. A while."

"But. . .you've never said anything before."

She stared at me. Her look was still accusative. She seemed to be mulling over my comment. "Up to now, everything's gone pretty good," she said. "I've had no complaints. Now I do."

"Oh."

"The food, well it could be better, but it's okay. Litter box, it's usually clean. Warm enough bed. But today you've put me in this cage and driven since before daylight, and if you don't know it, I've wet myself, and I think I may poop on myself in a few minutes, and this day may never end, and so I'd just like to know why. Why are you doing this?"

It was true what she said. In order to reach my daughter's home in Louisiana, I had left Kentucky very early, when the grass in my yard crackled with frost; and I had apparently forced Sundae into her cage before she did her morning eliminations. About two hours into the trip, someplace in deepest Tennessee, she began to moan, and I didn't know what was wrong. I had never heard her make such a sound. I was puzzled until I smelled the problem. I stopped at a service station, stole a roll of paper towels from the men's room, and sopped up her cage. Her fur was damp, and she looked at me in sullen rage. It was an hour later that she spoke.

I thought I was hallucinating. I do that sometimes, when I've gone too long without food, and it was now getting close to noon. I popped a chocolate candy puff into my mouth and chewed. I felt the sugar spreading out across my stomach and then through my bloodstream and to my brain. I waited for a minute before I spoke again, so I could find out whether she could talk with my sugar level higher. She could. "Why?" she repeated.

"You are in your cage because we are on a trip," I said tentatively.

"A trip? What's a trip?" She had never been on a trip before, except from the pound to my house and a couple of times to see the veterinarian.

"A. . .journey. We are going to visit my daughter, and she lives a long way off. It takes all day. That's just the way it is."

"Where is this place?"

"Louisiana. To see my daughter. I've talked to you a lot about her." Oddly, though I had no idea Sundae could talk, I had often talked to her, sharing my most intimate thoughts. I guess most people do that, expecting an animal to understand even if she can't talk, perhaps because she can't talk, can't tell others.

"You didn't ask me if I wanted to go."

"No, I didn't," I admitted. "But there was really no choice. You couldn't stay at home by yourself for a week, now could you?" I was talking to her like I would have talked to a child. I realized I really had gone around the bend.

"Why not?" she persisted.

"What if your food ran out?"

There was a long silence. I looked down and through the bars, and I could see the wheels in her brain turning. "I get the point," she finally agreed.

"So?" I said. I sort of enjoyed putting her in her proper place.

"Well, why do I have to stay in this cage?"

"For your own good. I've read that if a cat sees rapid movement all around, she can't process it, and she gets scared."

"Pretty paternalistic," she said. "Why do you treat me like a baby?"

I chose to ignore that question because I didn't want to admit that I was treating her like a human of any kind. "You see, if you were a dog, they say, I could let you sit up here on the seat beside me. But. . ." I paused. "You are not a dog."

She took a deep breath and sat up as tall as was possible in the cage. "I thank my lucky stars every day of my life for that," she said.

"I can't stop the car and walk you."

"Not on a leash, not like those slave animals called dogs," she agreed.

"So since I can't stop and let you take a whizz from a leash, you're stuck there. I can't let you do your business on my seat or the floor. This fabric cost a lot of money."

"You just let me do it on myself."

"Sorry about that."

"Why do we have to go on this trip?" she said.

"I want to see my daughter. She wants me to come and visit. Visits, family get-togethers, it's what people do at Christmas."

"Christmas?" she said, showing some interest.

"Yes. Christmas."

"I don't get it," she said, eyeing me suspiciously, as if I had mentioned some deep, dark mystery to which she had not been initiated. She could talk, but there were gaps in her knowledge. It was comforting to see that she didn't know everything. I would have to explain Christmas to her.

So that's how they began, my long series of heart-to-heart talks with my cat Sundae, talks in which we taught each other about life. I explained human things to her, and she explained feline things to me. Conversations with my cat.

I found Sundae in June of 1994. She was already two years old or so, she has never been willing to tell me her real age, but the Vet who first examined her for me estimated her to be about that age then. I had just returned from a year of study in England. My house, which had been vacant while I was gone, felt terribly empty. It even smelled empty. Friendships would take time to renew. Romances would take even longer. I could get a pet immediately, and immediately was when I needed to fill my house with companionship.

I didn't look in newspapers for ads. I didn't want anything with a pedigree. Since I don't have one myself, it seemed silly to have a pet with one. I didn't want my pet to be better bred than I am. I went to the Humane Shelter because I wanted an outcast, not a pet from a fresh litter with all sorts of potential takers, but an animal with perhaps only a few weeks to live unless I saved it from euthanasia. I'm an outcast myself, having been abandoned to fend for myself by a wife who went on to better things. The Shelter is the place to find pets that were accidents, or were hard to control, or who got in people's ways. I'm all three of those things; and I needed a pet to match me.

I went specifically looking for a cat. I've had dogs for pets, and I didn't want another one. Dogs, to be blunt, are dumb. I once read that owning a dog is like having a retarded brother-in-law living in your house. A dog is affectionate, sure, if that's what you value; but a dog is too "damp" with his affection. I prefer the cool, objective affection of a cat. A cat gives its affection only to select persons, at times it considers appropriate, and is able to save up its affection while you are gone to work without pining away. In fact, I think most cats enjoy their time away from you as much as you enjoy your time away from them. So—a cat.

Also I wanted a pretty cat, and that meant a calico. A calico has three colors, usually black, white, and orange, really pretty; and a calico is always, by genetic rule, a female. Since I've always preferred girls to boys in every species, a calico cat seemed the perfect choice.

I went to the Humane Shelter (they still call it The Pound where I live) with some trepidation. I knew there would be a variety of cats there, lots from which to choose. I knew that I would have to leave all but one behind. I knew that the shelf life for an animal at the Pound is about six weeks. The ones who are not claimed in that short time die. Sad but true.

A big, gruff man—who I discovered really had a heart as soft as his square shoulders were hard—led me to the cat pens. At first, as we walked, he told me I had a choice of fifty; and then when he learned I wanted a calico, he said there were about ten. They were grouped, each in its own cage, by color. He led me slowly down the row of cells, past the blacks and whites and grays and oranges. A hundred sets of eyes watched me. We came to the calicos, twenty eyes. Some of the younger ones flirted with me, hopping around, showing off, unable to contain their enthusiasm as they seemed to be demonstrating the happy life they could bring to me if I chose them. Others, older, more experienced, wiser, seemed to know the odds were against them and hardly moved a muscle, understanding that it would probably be a waste of energy to try to attract this shabby guy passing by them. One or two showed open contempt, letting me know that I just was not their kind of man. Then I saw Sundae.

She was in one of the lower cages, a bad sign, a bad place to be, probably passed over for a week or two, without much hope. She eyed me cynically. Too many fickle men had looked her over and gone on. But she was beautiful. Her face had black, white, and orange stripes. She had a white neck. Her eyes promised intelligence. I couldn't of course then guess that she would be the most remarkable creature I would ever meet. "How about this one?" I asked the boss.

My question brought him to a stop. He stood staring down at the lower cage, breathing heavily. I could smell a mixture of Old Spice and Lysol Disinfectant.

"Her?" he said.

"Yes. Wonder why nobody's taken her? She's a real knock-out."

"Guess 'cause she's not a kitten. Looks like she's got some miles on her. You wonta hold her? I can get 'er out for ya."

"Sure."

He squatted down and opened the cage, and she shied away from him. He reached a long, hairy arm inside, pulled her out, and held her away from his body while he gave her a once-over.

She was indignant at being treated that way, but she had apparently been there long enough not to argue too strenuously. She also seemed to know the man well enough to understand that he wouldn't let her disagree.

"She's got an eye infection," he said. "Most of 'em do. It's in the air in this place. You take her it'll cost you $15 to doctor it."

"That's all right," I assured him.

He tilted her backward and stared at her underside, rubbing a thumb through her hair. "She's been spayed." He felt of her front paws. "Declawed too. That's good."

"Is it?" I had always been told declawing wasn't such a good idea.

"If you want a house cat, you have to do it. Now it's been done, you'll have to keep her inside. We make you sign a promise. She can't defend herself clawless like that."

"Right." I had intended to keep her inside anyway. I've had had several cats hit by cars. I wanted this one to be with me for a long time.

"Ain't young."

"Me neither," I said.

The man and I laughed at that. The cat gave out a low, gutteral growl. Now that I think about it, she may have understood some English even then.

"Where did they find her?" I asked him, supposing she had been a stray, lost, and found by a person who brought her to the Shelter.

"She wadden lost," he said. "Man brought 'er in. Left 'er."

"Really?" I couldn't imagine why someone would do that, not to a beautiful creature like this one. I shook my head.

"Yep. Said they was moving. Said they wouldn't allow pets where his family was gonna live. Couldn't keep 'er."

"But. . ." I was stunned. Someone who had owned her, and it appeared had cared for her pretty well, had just dropped her off in this place where she would have no more than a few weeks to live.

He read my expression of surprise, repulsion, contempt.

"Yeah. Bad, huh? Happens all the time. They call this a throw-away society."

Well, that's all it took to convince me to take her home. Within half an hour I had put my $50 adoption fee on the table and signed a paper that I would be the owner, protector, guardian, and lover of this calico cat. I took her home and showed her how to find her food and litter box. Slowly she began coming out from under the couch for longer periods to explore the house, and we got to know each other. By the middle of her third day with me her name was Sundae.

Why Sundae? Search me. I didn't get her on a Sunday. She didn't look like any kind of Sundae I had ever seen in an ice cream shop. It just suited her. It was a pet's name, cute, yet it had a certain dignity about it. Sundae.

"I said, I don't get it," Sundae repeated when I didn't respond to her speculative probe for an explanation. She was spunky, I knew that. That first week she was with me she had fought me when I tried to doctor her eye with the gummy medicine squeezed out of a tube. Then she fought me when I had to feed her a pink medicine through a mouth dropper for an infection.

In fact, the morning that stuff was finally all gone, I held the dropper out to her to show her she wouldn't have to take it any-more, and she knocked it out of my hand. By the way, I learned from her swipe that she's a southpaw. I'm serious. She prefers to use her left paw. But I was a bit surprised when she was spunky enough to make me stay on the topic of Christmas.

"You don't get what?" I said. Right then it occured to me that most of my friends would declare me insane if I told them I was about to discuss the meaning of Christmas with my cat.

"You said people put their cats in cages and take trips that never seem to end because of this thing called Christmas." She pronounced the last word with a marked distaste. In her mind it was associated with bad times.

"Yes," I said, "people like to see each other at Christmas. Or at least they like to pretend that they do." I was trying to be honest. I wanted to tell her the truth. "A lot of people don't really want to go, and they know they're not wanted."

"Christmas," Sundae said. "It means getting together, a reunion."

"Your vocabulary is remarkable," I said with some admiration.

"Good thing you speak English," she said. "I hate to think what it would have been like if you had been Japanese and I'd of had to learn that."

"Right," I nodded. I wondered how she knew what Japanese sounded like. I learned later that she had been watching television. "But no, Christmas doesn't mean reunion. That just got associated with it somewhere along the way. Christmas actually means the day Jesus was born."

"Jesus?" She turned her head, the way she did when I thought she was thinking what to do next. She looked toward the back of her cage for a time before she turned back to me. "Is he the one with the beard? The blond?"

"Yes. How did you know?"

"Sometimes I watch that religious channel, usually on Sunday mornings, when you're still asleep. His picture pops up a lot."

That was the first time I knew she watched. I would later learn that she also watched during the day when I was at work.

"So he was born on Christmas," she said.

"Yes. At least that's what we are taught to believe. Jesus was born on Christmas Day in Palestine."

"Was it as cold there and then as it is here and now?"

"I don't know." I thought about it for a moment. I wasn't sure how far into this subject I wanted to go with her; but I decided to go a bit farther. "Actually, we don't know the real day. He was probably born in the spring."

"How do you know that?"

"Well, I don't. But judging by the holidays mentioned, it's likely."

"So why do you say it was in the winter?"

"I think December 25 was already some kind of holy day, before he was born, and a long time later, after they had forgotten exactly when he was born, they picked that day."

"Wait," she said, "You've confused me. Why didn't he set them straight about it?"

"He couldn't. He was dead."

"Oh. How old was he when he died?"

"Thirty-three, I think."

"How old would he be now? About your age?"

"No, no," I laughed. "He would be two thousand."

"What?" Her eyes were as large as saucers. She probably had trouble imagining someone as old as I was, let alone someone two thousand.

"I mean, he lived about two thousand years ago. That's one reason we don't really know what day his birthday was."

Her eyes narrowed. "So, you're telling me that this dude lived two thousand years ago——that's about 20,000 cats' lives——and yet people still remember him, still remember his birthday, even if they have the date wrong?"

"Well, a lot of people think he was a pretty great. . .what did you call him?. . .dude. A pretty great man."

"Do they think any other men are great?"

"Sure. There's Socrates. . ."

"Any women?"

"Joan of Arc. . ."

"Do you drive all day and night to visit people, and keep your cat in a cage the whole way, on the birthday of Socrates or Joan of Arc?"

"No."

"Why not? And why for Jesus?"

"A lot of people believe the others were good, great even, but they think Jesus was the Son of God. That's different."

"Oh." This time she didn't just turn her head, she turned her whole body, and her face disappeared from view. She has grey and black stripes down her sides and a tail like a raccoon. She switched her tail around as she thought about what I had said. Apparently I had made a big impression on her. Finally she began to shift and came back full circle. "So. . .because a little baby was born two thousand years ago in. . .what did you call that place?"

"Palestine. It's about ten thousand miles from here. In the part of the world they call the Middle East." I thought I would confuse her more. "He was born in a stable there."

"So was I," she said. Then she made a clicking sound, as if to indicate that this made her pretty important too. "That's odd for a human," she said. "Poor family?"

"They got to town during a convention."

She sniffed with contempt. "A baby, people believe to be the Son of God, and they made his parents stay in a stable." She sniffed again. "But back to the subject: A baby, born two thousand years ago, ten thousand miles from here, believed but not proven to be the Son of God, you don't know for sure what day he was born, and people this far away in time and space still go these great distances, with their cats in cages, to visit relatives, even though they don't enjoy going and the relatives don't enjoy having them."

"Yes," I had to admit. "That's true for a lot of people."

"Unbelievable," she said.

She grew quiet, and I decided not to say anything more, fearful that I would get her started asking more questions I couldn't answer, or if I could, the answers would just get her more upset and confused.

Cats are a thoughtful species. You've probably noticed how

they stare off into space, their mental wheels turning. William Faulkner believed that cats once ruled the earth but were smart enough to get rid of the job and foist it off onto a less intelligent breed, mankind. Now we humans do all the work and worry while cats just sit and think and eat.

Finally Sundae said: "Okay, now Jesus I know about. He has the blond beard. Looks like a concert guitarist. Wears a white night-gown. But what about the other dude?"

I wondered where Sundae had picked up the word dude. Not from me. I later learned that she had been watching MTV while I was at work.

"Other. . .dude?"

"Yes. He has a beard too, but his is grey. He looks pretty old. He's been on a lot just these last few weeks. Fat guy. Wears red."

"Oh," I smiled. "That's Santa Claus. Old Saint Nick."

"I see pictures of Jesus all the time, but I've only seen Nick the last few weeks."

"Yes," I said. "He's more seasonal."

"Is he a friend of Jesus?"

"Not really." Sundae was leading me into deep water, and I wondered how well I would be able to swim in it. "Not in this life anyway." She turned her head to one side, showing me her confusion, and I hurried on. "See, Santa Claus lived about sixteen hundred years ago, four hundred after Jesus. But he lived over in that same part of the world. He was a bishop."

"Bishop?"

"A leader of the church," I said. "He's famous, and admired, and we see a lot about him at Christmas, because he knew a poor man who had three daughters but no dowries. . ."

"Dowries? What is that?"

"Well, back then, a girl had to have money before a man would marry her."

"But not now?"

"No. Now it's the other way around. A man has to have money before a girl will marry him. It's changed."

"A man without money can't get married?"

"It happens. But if he wants to keep his wife, he has to get some quickly."

"You got married."

"Yes." I wondered how she knew. We had never discussed it. Maybe she had seen pictures on the wall and figured it out.

"Did you have money?"

"No. I lucked out."

"Did you make some quickly?"

"No."

"That's why you're no longer married?"

"Yes."

"I see." And I think by the way she looked at me with such pity she did.

"Anyway," I said, wanting to get beyond this part of the conversation, "Nicholas went to the man's house three different nights, and each night he pitched a little bag of gold over the back fence into his yard. So that way each daughter got a dowry, and each one could get married. See those packages on the seat above you?"

Sundae craned her neck and looked up at the fancily wrapped boxes. "Yes, barely, but I can see them," she said.

"Well, they're gifts I'm taking to family members, to imitate Saint Nick, who imitated God, who gave the world his son Jesus. That's why Nicholas is big around Christmas time. Each of the presents we give each other is like a little bag of gold. He taught us the real spirit of Christmas. It's supposed to give you pleasure to give someone else a gift.

"Did you have fun buying them?"

"Honestly? No, not really."

"Why?"

"The stores were crowded. People were rude. Everything cost too much. I bought all these things because I was ashamed not to."

"So that's why Nick is everywhere now. He reminds you to buy things for people, even though you hate doing it and do it only because you're ashamed not to."

"Yep."

"But I guess at least people like to get the gifts, like those young girls who needed the dowry from Nicholas."

"I'm not even sure of that," I said. "Most of the time I get the feeling I never buy the right thing and people don't like what I gave them."

"So you buy out of shame and buy the wrong things. Wonder what Nicholas thinks about the way he's being used."

"Used?"

"Used. I've seen him drinking Coca Cola, trying on tennis shoes, even stuffing cigars into a stocking. He's used all right."

"I guess you're right. To answer the question, I guess he wouldn't be very proud of the whole thing, would he?"

"Then why does he agree to pose?"

I realized that while Sundae understands a lot of things well, chronology is not one of her strong subjects. "Oh, Nicholas doesn't do that. Those are actors pretending to be him."

"But the photographs, they're really Nicholas, aren't they?"

"Photographs? Oh, there aren't any photographs of Nicholas . . .or Jesus either. People just guess what they looked like."

"So Nicholas wasn't necessarily a fat little guy in a red suit? Jesus wasn't necessarily a blond dude in a night gown?"

"Nope. In fact, the pictures of them we see mostly represent the way they were portrayed by modern painters. Jesus looks like an Italian, and Nicholas looks Dutch."

Sundae was silent for a long time, digesting what I had said, before she finally spoke: "Let me get it all straight," she said, "A baby was born two thousand years ago ten thousand miles from here in a stable. People decided he was the Son of God, God's gift to man. Then four hundred years after that Nicholas the Bishop put on a red suit and threw gold over a poor man's wall to help his daughters get married, giving in the same spirit God gave Jesus. And now they use these two men to make people feel so guilty that they spend money buying things that no one wants for people who buy for them only because they too feel guilty if they don't."

"I guess so."

"And on top of that, in order to deliver the gifts you didn't want to buy to those people who don't really want them, you put your poor cat in a cage and drive until she wets herself."

"Yes, and I receive gifts from people that I don't want because they feel guilty not to buy them for me."

"Huh!"

Sundae turned away from me again. All I could see was her orange-and-black-striped rump.

I wondered what she was doing. She seemed to have understood everything pretty well. What she was doing, I was soon to discover, was waxing philosophical. After about forty miles and half an hour, she turned to face me.

"It's a sad state of affairs, what you've told me, James," she said. I found it comfortingly familiar, the way she called me by my given name.

"Well," I sighed. "That's life. At least as we know it here and now."

"I like the stable story—-and the fat guy and his gold bags—-but what started out nice has really turned weird."

"I know."

"I hate to see good things get all twisted."

"Me too."

"Still. . .I guess you humans might have messed things up even worse if it weren't for those two dudes."

"You think so?"

"I do. Without them you wouldn't know anything at all about gifts. You would probably keep all your money for yourselves. You would probably never go to visit your children or your parents. That would be even worse than this farce we're living out." She nodded slowly, savoring her conclusions. She was sure she had human beings figured out. She didn't know at that point how much more she had to learn about us, how much more weird she would find us to be. "Even a gift that is squeezed out of you by guilt, one no one really wants, is better than no gift at all. Even a visit you don't want to make, to someone who dreads having you, is better than no visit at all."

"Not a pretty picture, Sundae."

"No, it's not. But it could be worse. Without Jesus and Nicholas you humans would be the most selfish, lonely creatures on the face of the earth."

"So you don't object to the cage."

"I didn't say that. I hate it. In fact, stop when you can. I need to find me a nice, sandy spot and take my time over it."

"But I don't have a leash."

"I wouldn't walk on one if you did. Just stop and let me out."

"What if you run away?"

"Where are we?"

"Mississippi." We had crossed the state line while she was waxing philosophical.

"Would I run away here? Do you think I would want to live the rest of my life in Mississippi? I've seen it on television."

"So if I let you out loose, you won't leave me."

"No. I want to be there when those people open all these boxes full of things they don't want. That will be fun."

20

Then she laughed. The laugh started low in her throat, like her growl, and grew louder and higher until it sounded almost human. I was stunned. I didn't know Sundae could laugh.

Did I tell you?   Sundae is my cat.

NEW YEAR'S DAY

Two weeks went by before Sundae and I had another extended conversation. We talked off and on, in snatches, bits and pieces, during our time in Louisiana; but we had to be careful not to let anyone hear us. If news had escaped that we were carrying on conversations, I would have been sent to an asylum or she would have been sold to a carnival. So we conversed, but always briefly, only when something important came up, while we were away from home. We were both relieved when we got back to Kentucky, to our home, and could talk openly.

We got back on December 29, driving the last hundred miles in a snowstorm; and we were both so nervous and exhausted that we went to separate rooms of the house and didn't have much to say to each other for a couple of days. It was on New Year's Day that we resumed the philosophical business we had pursued on the trip to Louisiana.

New Year's Day dawned clear, sunny actually, full of hope and promise. The only clouds in my sky were from the headache I nursed, and that came from the wine I had drunk with friends the night before. I drank pot after pot of coffee and made phone call after phone call, sitting in a bean-bag chair, as Sundae sat on her perch and looked out the window at the sunshine on the snow. Occasionally she would look back at me, listen for a time to my side of a conversation, yawn, and go back to her window. She swished her tail from side to side when a bird flew by.

Finally I made my last call, put down the telephone on the floor, and closed my throbbing eyes to rest. I may have dozed off. The next sound was Sundae clearing her throat. "Why all the calls?" she said. I opened my eyes and squinted against the light coming through her window. She jumped down and crossed to the bed, jumped up on it, and stretched out facing me. She was considerate to go where I didn't have to face the sun. "Huh?" she said.

"The calls?"

"Yes. For someone as stingy as you are, you're sure using up a lot of money making so many telephone calls today."

I chuckled. It hurt to laugh, so I didn't do it again. "It's New Year's," I sighed.

"It is?"

I was just a bit surprised that she was puzzled. I guess I thought she knew everything. After all, she watched television, that much I had learned during the past week. I assumed she had watched the ball fall in Times Square the night before.

"Yeah. This is the first day of 1995. We're in a brand new year."

"How can you tell?"

"By the calendar. It's something people agree on. January first is always the beginning of a new year. This one is about the nineteen hundred and ninety-fifth since the birth of Christ."

"You said about. . . You're not sure?"

"It's a guess. Like December 25 is a guess, you remember, about Christmas. It was around that year when Jesus was born. It's been about 1995 years, but that's not known for sure. Actually, some people say we missed it by about six years."

"Which way?"

"He may have been born six years earlier."

"So this would be. . ." She calculated. "This is maybe twenty-oh-one?"

"Might be."

"Huh. People are not very precise."

"No." I closed my eyes again and tried to ease the pain. "But it's a nice day. Sunshine. No precipitation. That's a good sign."

"Why?"

I opened my eyes. "They say. . ."

"Who say. . .?"

"They. People. It's collective human wisdom."

She yawned.

"They say that what happens on the first day of the year will be repeated consistently through the rest of the year. The year 1995 should have lots of sunny days. Not just the weather, but it should be a good year for living. I expect it to be a wonderful year."

"Dream on," she yawned again. "But you didn't answer my question. Why are you making all of these calls?"

"It's a tradition. You're supposed to get in touch with everyone who's important to you on New Year's Day. Family, friends, former wives. . ."

"Why?"

"You wish them good health and good luck. They wish you good health and good luck. They say it brings good health and good luck to be wished good health and good luck by people who care about you."

"They again. Collective human folk wisdom, right?"

"Yes." Once more I closed my eyes, and this time I rubbed my temples. It felt good, and I sighed deeply. Maybe by nightfall I would feel all right.

"You sick?"

"Headache. I drank too much last night."

"Too much?"

"Wine. Remember I was gone? I went to a New Year's Eve Party. There was plenty to drink and I didn't know when to stop. I have a hangover."

"What you drank gave you a headache?"

"Yep." I looked at her, hoping to find some sympathy, but all she did was shake her head with contempt. "It's a tradition," I said defensively.

"They say to do it?"

"Yes."

"Yesterday you did everything you could to make yourself sick. Today you call people to get them to wish you good health. You humans and your logic."

"Tradition."

"You want every day of the year to be as good as the first, so you make sure that you will be sick that day. Do you want to be sick all of 1995?"

"I've made a resolution not to drink during 1995. Not as much anyway."

"A resolution? Like the ones Congress makes on C-SPAN? That won't do you very much good, if your resolution is like theirs."

"It's another tradition. You are supposed to make New Year's Resolutions. Make a list of things you want to do differently in the next year. I've made seven for this year. One is not to drink so much wine."

"What are the others?"

I picked up the pad I had written on and let drop to the floor during my calls. I read the seven off to her. Among them was a resolution to diet, to write more poetry, to keep the house a bit cleaner. As I read it, I realized that my ambitions had been severely curtailed in recent years. Once I would have resolved to publish a book and build a new house. I had become more realistic.

"Nothing about your cat?" Sundae said. She flashed me a lopsided smile.

"What about my cat?"

"Oh, maybe a better brand of food? Maybe a new window box? Maybe a promise never to take me to the Vet again, especially for a dip."

Sundae hated dips. She always returned from dips angry. She

would scratch herself for days and look at me with malice.

"Maybe I'll add another resolution."

"Let me know when you decide to do it. I'll help with the wording."

"Okay," I promised. Slowly I got to my feet, taking it in stages, prepared to fall back into my chair if my head started to pop. It didn't, and I felt I could move. I shuffled across the floor toward the kitchen. Sundae got up, stretched, jumped off the bed, and followed me.

I cut open a sack of blackeyed peas and poured them into my crock pot, filled it with water, and flipped on the switch. Then I took a frozen hog jowl out of the refrigeraor and began cutting it up.

"That smells good," Sundae said. "Is it for me?"

"This? No, it's for me. It wouldn't be good for you."

"So you know what's good and what's not good for me?" She looked up at me accusatively. "What arrogance!"

"I'm saving you from a coronary thrombosis. If I let you eat fat meat, you may have a better looking coat, but you'll die young of a heart attack."

"And you won't?"

"I will, but I've got more years to spare than you have."

"Huh! They say I have more lives than you."

"They?" I teased.

She watched as I dropped the fat meat into the pea juice and shook various forms of flavoring into the pot. Finally she spoke: "You're going to eat that?"

"I'm not sure," I admitted. "Right now I couldn't; but maybe by the time it's boiled for three or four hours, my stomach will be able to handle it."

"What is it?"

"It's blackeyed peas and hog jowl. Another tradition. It's

something people eat on New Year's Day. It brings good fortune."

"But not good health."

"Well, they say it does, along with good fortune."

"They say that too, huh?"

"Yes, the ubiquitous they."

Having set my pot to cook, I made my way back to my bean-bag chair. Peas in the pot, beans in my chair, I lived among the foods of my childhood. Not much had changed. Only now I owned a cat who could talk.

She followed me back. Some days she follows me everywhere I go, and others I hardly see her at all. This was one of her days to stick to me like glue. I could tell she hadn't satisfied herself about the New Year's Day business.

She stretched out on my bed again and looked at me intently. Once more I could see the wheels turning in her head. I wonder how cats are wired. Certainly not like humans, not like dogs either, they are a breed unto themselves. If there is, as some say, a single Creator of the world, He or She or It must have had fun creating all the variety around us. Cats, I think, must have been one of the last to be created. The Creator had a lot of experience by that time. The cat is a great idea.

"You told me December 25 was the birthday of Jesus."

"That's the day we celebrate it."

"Okay. And we start numbering the years from his birth."

"Except we're a few years off, probably."

"You're missing my point!" she huffed. I had upset her. "Even if both are off, shouldn't the first day of the year be when you celebrate his birthday? But it's a week later. Why?" Sundae is able to see every discrepancy in human logic and habit and tradition, yet she can't learn to spit up hair balls into her litter box. I find the ropey things all over the house. See what I mean about the way a cat's mind is wired?

"Well, yes, I suppose you're right. Maybe we just can't fit everything we want to do into one day, I don't really know."

She thought about this for a time. I was glad for the space of quiet, to let my head rest. Conversations with Sundae can be tiring, even when you're not hung over, and I was.

"All human beings recognize this day, a week after Jesus' birthday, as the first day of a New Year? All over the world?"

Now she was opening a new can of worms. "No, not everyone," I sighed. "In Asia, China, Japan, places over there, they have New Year in another month or so."

"Why?"

"Something to do with the moon. The first full moon comes in late January or early February, and they start the year then." I waited for her to respond, but she just stared at me. I knew I should have left well enough alone, but I couldn't help going on. "Then there are the Jews. . ."

"The what?"

"The other religion in this country. The Jewish people celebrate New Year in the autumn. Its because of their religious tradition."

"The Jews? Are they the ones who wear the beanies to church?"

"They don't call them beanies, and they go to synagogue, not church, but. . . Wait a minute. How did you know that?"

"I watch Rabbi Marc Gelman on "Good Morning America."

"Oh. Yes, I guess you would."

"You know, he and Father Thomas Hartman are always discussing religious topics. But I'm puzzled. How are the Jews different from the Christians? That's what you are, isn't it, a Christian? I know you celebrate Christmas. The rabbi celebrates Hannakuh."

"I guess I'm a Christian. I don't think I'm a very good one."

"Because you drink too much wine?"

"That and other things I do."

"Why don't you resolve to do better?"

"I am, didn't I tell you?"

"Okay, but I still don't know how Jews are different from Christians. Jews and Christians look the same. In fact, I think Rabbi Gellman looks a lot like Jimmy Swaggart." Sundae's tastes in religious programming were broad.

"What? I don't think they look alike at all."

"Sure they do. But then all you humans look alike. You're not like cats. Look at all the variety there is among us."

"Well, with Jews and Christians, it's not anything physical. Well, it might be, but you don't need to know about that. It's mostly just a difference of belief."

"What difference?"

"To the Jewish people, Jesus was a good man but not the Son of God."

"But didn't the rabbi say one morning that Jesus was Jewish?"

"That's right, he was."

"So Jews doubt one of their own was the Son of God and non-Jews believe he was?"

"Yes."

"Humans!" She stood up and turned several times in a circle before she lay back down and blew out a heavy, pungent Purina breath. She stared at me for a long time. "Why hasn't someone come up with the idea of having New Year in the spring?" she said.

"Spring?"

"Yes. Think about it. The year is like a life, isn't it? Spring comes, things are born and begin to grow. There's this wonderful period of being young. Then they reach maturity and go through a hot summer of survival, followed by slow decline through the autumn, when leaves fall like your hair is falling; and then comes winter when things die. Why have New Year during this time we're in now? Why not have New Year at the new part of the year?"

"It makes sense. Some people believe Jesus was born in the spring, judging by the holidays going on when he was born."

"Well then. . ."

"I know. But you can't reverse tradition. This is the way it is, and it won't change, no matter how logical and sane the idea is."

"Because humans reign."

"You got it."

The first waft of blackeyed peas and hog jowl reached us about that time. Sundae perked up and took a deep breath. "Smells good to me," she said.

" But it's just for me."

"Yes, that's just about as sensible as the rest of this day," she said. "You call New Year a day in the middle of death. You go out and drink until you have a headache, come home and resolve never again to drink so much, not until the next time anyway. You cook unhealthy food that's supposed to bring you good health, and you pray that by the time it's done your stomach will be able to take it. You make phone calls to people who wish you good luck, and you wish them good luck, but you know the calls won't bring you good luck. You write down promises to be a better person in the future than you were in the past, knowing that you probably won't change and that you'll have to make the same promises next year. All quite human."

"You don't think much of the human race, do you?"

She thought about it for a moment. "I think New Year is a lot like Christmas."

"How?"

"It's a good idea, but you've scrambled it all around. It could be so much better, and I don't know how you could have got it so confused. On the other hand, without it you might be a lot worse than you are now. Like Christmas."

"How so?"

"You might never call your friends. You might never stop drinking and think about life. You might never even try to do better. You might eat hog jowl every day instead of confining it to one day a year." She looked at me, and I'll swear she winked. "And without it I wouldn't have half the number of laughs I get. Thank you, my human, for entertaining me so royally. You know you really make my life complete."

Sundae is my cat.

SAINT VALENTINE'S DAY

Sundae is ambivalent about affection. She is nothing like a dog. Dogs generally are ready to share affection at any moment, in any place, for any reason. I suppose that is why they are such favorites of insecure people, people who need constant reassurance that someone loves them. You can treat a dog any old way, neglect him, forget to feed him, scold him, and all it takes to have him slobbering over you with unquestioning love is to whistle him to come. Not so with cats. They have sensitive natures and long memories. Especially my cat Sundae.

Not only does she not forget a rare misstep on my part, but she also goes through various stages in her willingness to grant me her favors. Sometimes for several days she will run to the door when I come home, rub against my leg as I fix my dinner, sit in my lap while I read, even rub her moist nose against my cheek. Then, for no reason I can see, she will turn cold, refuse to touch me, even spend most of her time in a room as far from me as she can find.

Unless she is really angry with me, she usually likes to sit in my lap while I watch television, but even then she seldom faces me. She lies stretched down my lap, facing the screen. Of course now that she talks to me I know that she watches the programs because she tells me what she thinks of various actors and athletes; but I think it is more than that: I think she prefers her intimacy to be somewhat objective.

For a long time I wondered if Sundae loved me. She obviously didn't love anyone else. She generally avoided my human visitors, although usually once during each visit she would walk slowly through the room where we were talking, just to let us see her and comment on how pretty she was. I knew she hated other cats, especially the ones that came up on the porch and hissed back and forth with her through screened windows. She was operated on, before I found her, to make sure she would never respond to the lure and howls of male cats. She thinks of me as her only companion, and in that way I knew she cared what happened to me. Whether this was love or just dependency, I didn't know. I didn't even know whether I loved her—I thought maybe what I felt for her was just dependency as well. On Valentine's Day I got some answers.

Early in February I started to receive little cards wishing me a happy Valentine's Day. Some of them were from mere friends, all women, who know I'm a bachelor and feel sorry for me and worry that I might not be remembered on the Day of Love. I got one from my daughter, lighthearted, the kind that says "I love you" without sounding too serious about it. Three or four came from former sweethearts, going all the way back to high school and extending through the previous year, cards that expressed nostalgia about what had been, what might have been, what still might be were I not the man I am. One or two were joke cards, more insulting than affectionate, neither of them signed, from my students I guessed.

Although Sundae can understand what I say and what she hears on radio and television, she can't read. She seems to enjoy looking over my mail, however, and she apparently can distinguish between papers and magazines, junk advertising, and personal letters. She noticed all of the strangely shaped envelopes, mostly red in color, that were coming. It was a Saturday morning, and she was lying in her bed next to where I sat reading the morning paper, when she asked me about them.

"Is it close to Christmas again?" she said.

"No. Christmas is nearly a year away. We only have one Christmas each year; and you remember that came in December. It's February now."

"I thought so."

"Why do you ask?"

"No reason."

"Oh. Well, something must have made you think of it. You haven't seen Saint Nicholas on television, have you?"

"No. But people seem to be remembering you."

"Remembering me?" I honestly didn't know what she meant. The cards didn't come in clumps. I had been getting maybe one a day or one every other day, and since I didn't take any of them very seriously, I hadn't thought much about Valentine's Day.

"You've been getting a lot of little cards. It just reminds me of that time just before Christmas when you got a lot of them."

"Oh," I said. "Cards. Yes, well I did get Christmas cards then. The ones I'm getting now are called Valentines. It'll soon be Valentine's Day."

"So that's what they've been advertising on television. But wait. People are supposed to buy candy and flowers."

"Some people do. But the ones who send me something don't feel I'm worth high-priced gifts. A card is good enough for me, they say."

"Candy and flowers cost more than cards?" Sundae said.

"Yes. Quite a bit."

It sometimes surprises me what Sundae knows and what she doesn't know. I keep forgetting that she doesn't understand money, prices, costs. She might, for example, know that a certain kind of cat food tastes better than another, but it never occurs to her that there is any difference in price between the two. She doesn't understand, fortunately, that while some pedigreed cats might cost a thousand dollars I only paid fifty for her at the Shelter.

"Who sends these cards to you?" she asked.

"People who want me to know, or at least think, they love me."

She sat up in her bed, as if I had just said something significant. "What is love?" she said with a raised eyebrow. It made me think of the way Pontius Pilate, in some Bible film I watched as a boy, asked, "What is truth?"

34

"Love?" I chuckled. "What a question. The greatest minds in the history of philosophy have asked that question; and I doubt that anyone has been able to answer it."

"Why?"

"It's. . .complex."

"Complex? What does that mean?"

"I guess it means love is so hard to describe that no one is smart enough to tell us what it really is."

"Even Socrates?"

"I'm not sure he even tried."

"How about Nicholas?"

"He showed us, but he didn't write a book on it. I guess we just have to watch what he did and try to learn from it."

"Love." She seemed to be tasting the word. It still didn't make much sense to her. "So you humans have a day in the year for love."

"Well, we're supposed to love all the time, but the kind of lives we live, we don't get around to it much, I guess, so yes, we have a day to say we love each other."

"Odd."

"Yes. You know human nature."

"I'm beginning to, boy, I'm beginning to." That line came right out of a television show we had watched together the week before. " Valentine? Is that the word?"

"Yes."

"Back at the Shelter, there was a big orange cat across the aisle from me with that name. He wasn't very friendly. All he would tell us was his name."

"Well, this day is named for another Valentine. Saint Valentine. He lived in Rome, during the third Christian century, and he was martyred for his faith."

"Martyred?"

"Killed. The government killed him because he insisted on believing in Jesus, and that was an unpopular thing in those days."

"In those days, huh?" Sundae said. "Times have changed. I get the impression it's unpopular now not to believe in him."

"Some places. Anyway, either Valentine was killed on February 14 or they just picked that day later on, we don't really know, but February 14 got to be the feast day of Saint Valentine, and that's the reason we send what we call 'valentines' to each other on that day."

"A valentine says you love someone."

"That's right."

"So Saint Valentine was a great lover. How many women did he knock off?"

"What? No, not that. In fact, I've read that the saint himself had nothing to do with all this love business, the cards, flowers, and candy, the I-Love-You stuff."

"No?"

"No, we call the cards valentines because we send them on Saint Valentine's Day; but I once read that this practice got started in the middle ages because people believed February 14 was the day wild birds mated."

"What? The day birds mated? What do birds have to do with love? I've never seen or heard a bird that sounded very loving."

"Oh, birds have always been associated with love. Haven't you ever heard of the birds and the bees?"

"No. Bees have to do with love? Ha! That's a laugh. If you think birds are mean, watch out the window when the bees come by. I saw them take out after a little boy on a bicycle. . ."

"I know, I know. But spring is the time you begin to see birds and bees, and that is the time boys and girls start to feel romantic. I guess that's why we say when you talk to a young person about love we call it a talk about the birds and the bees."

"Weird. No wonder humans are so confused."

"Especially about love."

"Especially. But you said it was a long time after Saint Valentine that they started calling his day the day of love. You said the middle. . ."

"Middle ages. They were a time when romance was born."

"Romance? Is that the same thing as love?"

"That's what people then began to say. Up until then the two had not been considered the same. But when rich young men began singing songs of love to rich young women, and when they started sending them love letters on the day birds mated, then they called it romance."

"So romance means singing love songs and writing love letters? Like the love letters you have been getting?"

"Vaguely."

"Anyone been singing to you? Or you to them?"

"Fat chance."

"Well, romance sounds pretty good to me. You tell people you love them, they tell you they love you. Not bad. Better than war."

"What do you know about war?"

"I watch The War Channel."

"Of course. Anyway, in the middle ages the rich young men and women invented romance. Pictures drawn during that time are full of these young people in the fields, among the birds and bees, in the early spring, romancing each other."

"Sounds nice."

"I guess. But then romance filtered down to everyone, even the people who had to work for a living, and that's when things got sort of messy."

"What do you mean?"

"Well, everyone came to believe that you're supposed to marry the person you romance, the person you love."

"Came to believe? They didn't always?"

"No. Through most of human time marriage was a kind of business arrangement. The man brought home the bacon, and the woman had the babies. They didn't feel like they had to feel romantic about it."

"Is romance bad for marriage?"

I knew I was in deep water here. Nothing I say about marriage sounds right. I wasn't very good at it myself, so I'm no expert. "Well, it is if people start to think they should marry only the person they feel romantic about. Then the romance dies, and they can't live together anymore. Love and romance maybe are just for the idle rich."

"Is that what happened to you?"

"No. I'm neither idle nor rich."

"Come on! Is that what happened to your marriage?"

Sundae is inordinately nosey about my marriage. I think she sometimes wonders if my wife will return and take her place in my life. Fat chance!

"I guess so. I fell in love. I wrote poems and love letters. I sang songs. I felt romantic. Then I got married, and then the romance wore off. If we had made marriage a business deal, it might have lasted."

"So let me get this straight." Sundae was looking me right in the eyes now, the way she always does when she wants to get something straight. "Humans fall in love. They romance each other. They marry each other. The romance dies. They separate, all hurt and brokenhearted, and they live pitiful lives, like yours."

"Well, some of us do. Others repeat the process. They keep falling in love, marrying, separating."

"Now that is dumb."

"Is that a compliment to my intelligence?"

"You're smart, but you're pitiful."

That really hurt, and I made an ugly face at her and went back to my reading. I raised the paper so that she couldn't see my face because there were tears in my eyes. Of all the holidays in the year, I find Valentine's Day the hardest. I'm a modern man. I was taught to believe that even we peasants can fall in love and marry the person we love. I would have hated it if my mother had chosen a good, solid housewife for me and I had made a business-deal marriage. Yet if that had happened, as in the old days among us peasants, I might not be alone now. I pretended to read, for a long time, until Sundae said something that caused me to lower my page.

"Do you love me, James?" she asked.

"What?" I said, shocked. "Do I love you?"

"Sometimes you sing to me, but you never send me flowers, or candy, or even a card. So do you really love me?"

"Do I feel romantic about you?"

"Yes."

"No. I've never seen much future to interspecies romances."

I was trying to be funny, but she didn't catch the humor. She just kept staring into my eyes, waiting for an answer. Did I love her?

"Well, yes, Sundae. I love you. I pet you and sweet-talk you and feed you and clean up after you, my messy little friend. I give you a warm house to live in, rent-free, and even when I'm gone I have Marsha from next door to drop in to make sure you're well. I think that's love. I sort of wish I had someone who loved me that much." I paused and watched her digest this information. "Compared to that family that gave you away. . ."

She looked at me sharply, and I saw the same expression in her eyes that she had probably seen in mine when she brought up the business about my marriage. I had never before mentioned the people who dropped her off at the Shelter, knowing that if she were not adopted in six weeks she would die.

"They didn't even tell me they were leaving town," she said.

She sighed. "They just put me in a cage one morning, left me there at the meat factory with all those other abandoned cats, and went on to their new life."

"Kind of like what my wife did to me."

"I apologize for bringing that up."

"I apologize for mentioning your first family."

"Let's forget it."

"Fine with me. Unless you want to talk about it."

"No. I don't," she said.

We sat looking at each other for a long time. I wondered what was going through that feline brain. It was beyond my penetration. All through our conversation she had sat in front of me on the bed, staring into my eyes. Finally she shook herself, as if to emerge from a trance, and lay down on her stomach facing me.

"So you believe you love me because you took me here to live, and you show your love by taking care of me all the time."

"I guess so. I think so."

"So that's what love is."

"Probably. It's not all the candy and flowers and cards, all that colored paper stuff. It's being responsible for someone. I know that without me you would be in trouble, so I take responsibility for you. Ergo, I love you." She showed no sign that she caught my use of Latin, so once more, to break the seriousness, I tried a little humor. "Without me, what would you be?"

She just stared at me. It made me nervous, her staring, and I decided to ask the question that had been on my mind for a long time. "Sundae, do you love me?"

She took a long time to answer. Then slowly she began to nod. At last she spoke: "I don't sing you songs. I don't buy you flowers or candy or send you cards. But I stay here with you. According to that Vet on television, I make you healthier by giving you companionship. You will live longer because of me. I have taken responsibility for you. So, yes, it would seem by our definition, I do love you."

Once more I felt tears come to my eyes. I don't know whether it was a distortion caused by the water on my lenses, but I would have sworn I saw Sundae smile. She got up and came over to the edge of the bed and jumped across into my lap. She rubbed against my chest and looked up into my eyes, still smiling, or so it appeared to me. She had not laughed at my humor, but she apparently had understood it. She turned mine on me. "Without me," she said, "what would you be?"

Sundae is my cat.

PRESIDENTS' DAY

You have doubtless guessed by now that I am a teacher. What other type person would talk with a cat and write about it? It is probably obvious also that I teach history because my cat Sundae and I are always talking about how things got the way they are, which is what history is. As a matter of fact, Sundae often asks me about things other than history, but I don't record those conversations because they show how limited my knowledge is about everything else. I know almost nothing about current events. I am Epimethean, which means I look only backward.

I was able to shine—but as usual also got shown up for some of my ignorance—when Sundae and I talked one day in February about American presidents. We had suffered through a cold winter, with lots of ice and snow, and for a wonderful change it was a bright, sunny day. I had no classes that day because my school had given us the holiday set aside to remember presidents. It fell between February 12, which was once celebrated as Lincoln's Birthday, and February 20, which was once celebrated as Washington's. It came of course on a Monday, and since I had caught up on all my sleep over the weekend, I got up early and began cleaning house, something I had not done since Thanksgiving.

Sundae watched me for a long time as I vacuumed, scrubbed, and collected the debris in a large plastic sack to be taken to the curb. She even followed me around for awhile, from room to room, until finally she settled back on her bed for her mid-morning nap. It was only when I stopped for a lunch snack that she roused herself, came into the kitchen, and took the other dining room chair, across the table from me. I could tell by the way she stared at me that she had something on her mind.

"What?" I said finally. "What is it?"

She blinked slowly, her large almond-shaped eyes disappearing and reappearing. She licked her lips. "Just wondering, why are you here?"

"Why am I here? Gal, you are philosophical today. Why are you here? Why is anyone here? What is the purpose of the human race, the feline species? What is the meaning. . ."

She shook her head in exasperation. "No, no, James. I don't mean why were you put on earth. I mean, why are you here, sitting in that chair, in this house, today? Isn't this Monday? Good Morning America was on today, so this is not Saturday or Sunday."

"You're right," I said. "It's Monday." Sundae waited for me to go on, but I was chewing and I decided to let her wait. She was impatient. "So why are you at home today?" she said.

"Does that bother you?"

"Yes, it does," she admitted. You're always here two straight days, Saturday and Sunday, and I have adapted to that. It interferes with my schedule some, but I know it's coming after five days of blissful solitude through the day. Now this is Monday, and for the third day you're here. The question is not difficult and not philosophical. Just tell why you're at home on Monday."

"Easy," I sniffed. "It's Presidents' Day."

"What does that mean? You have a day off work because of Bill Clinton?"

"No, because of past presidents. Maybe he will be part of it one day, when he leaves the White House, but not now."

"So you have a day to celebrate the fact that all the ones who have come before him have finally left office?"

"No, no. We just have a day to remember them, remember what they did, sort of honor their service to the country. But most of all we remember George Washington and Abraham Lincoln. They are the two we honor the most."

"Is this their birthday, like Christmas is the birthday of Jesus?"

"Close. Actually Lincoln's birthday was last week, and Washington's is next week. We used to get both days off, but finally, I guess because we were getting too many holidays too close together, they combined them. And it always comes on a Monday so we can have a three-day weekend."

"So it's neither Washington's nor Lincoln's birthday, it's both."

"Yep."

"Typical human logic."

I broke the last piece of bacon from my sandwich into two pieces and put one in front of Sundae. She sniffed it and let it lie on the table.

"Don't worry," I said. "I'll be at work tomorrow. You'll have your precious time alone back."

"Good," she said. "But you say Washington and Lincoln are the two top presidents, right? Why is that? What did they do?"

"Well," I said, pushing my chair back from the table. I love to be asked historical questions.

"Washington was the first president. He's sometimes called the Father of Our Country."

"He is? Because he had a lot of children?"

"No, actually he never had any."

"Why not? Too busy to get married?"

"No, he had a wife. A very loving one, it's said. And she had children by her first husband, who died. No, some people believe George was sterile."

"What is sterile?"

"He couldn't. . .have children. See, he had a major bout with mumps when he was a boy, and they may have 'gone down' on him. Thus, he fired blanks."

She studied my face and chose to ignore both my grin and the humor I was hoping to convey. The students in my classes always laugh at that joke, but not Sundae. "So you're saying that just because he was first, got to the presidency before anyone else, he's a top president? Being first is that important to humans?"

"In a way. But it's more than that. When you're first you get to start things, create things, make things work. Washington decided on the cabinet system, naming certain people to assist him in special areas. He rejected the idea that the president should be a king. He even had a say about the language we speak."

"What? English?"

"Yes. Since we had fought England for our independence and France had helped us, there were some who said we should make French our national language. Washington, who wasn't very good learning languages, discouraged that kind of talk."

"Hmmm," Sundae said. "I'm sorry about that. I've been watching the French lessons on television, and I think French would be easier for cats than English. The French all sound like us."

"Some people wanted us to speak German, but again the president disagreed."

Sundae stiffened. "Thank God for for George Washington."

"Yes. Well, anyway, for all his shortcomings, and there were some, we consider good old George the first among several great presidents. He wasn't much of a writer or political philosopher, not like Jefferson and Madison, and he couldn't speak very well, partly because he wore false teeth. And he was known to chase the girls a bit too much, especially as he got old."

"He reminds me a lot of Bill Clinton."

"Except the false teeth."

"Yes. What about Lincoln?"

"I don't think he wore false teeth."

"No, I mean, why is he tops?"

"Well, he became president at the most important time in our history, just as the Civil War broke out. He was able to keep the nation together, to keep it from dividing forever into little pieces. He saved the Union."

"How did he do that?"

"He fought a war."

"Oh yes," she said, nodding sagely. "I've seen it on The War Channel. The two sides wore blue and grey, right?"

"Right. Lincoln's side wore blue."

"They ran across fields at each other, yelling and waving blades, and they all died."

"Not all."

"Not all, but a lot, or so it looks to me."

"Yes. A lot."

"So since Lincoln's men killed a lot of people, they saved the Union."

"Something like that."

"What does the other side think of him?"

"Oddly enough, they like him too."

"Humans!"

"But he did more than save the Union. He also freed the slaves."

"The what?"

"The slaves. You see, before Mr. Lincoln became president, most of the black people in this country were slaves, they were owned by white people."

"Owned?"

"Like I own. . ." I caught myself just in time. I almost said like I owned Sundae. That would have been a mistake. She would never admit I owned her. If anything, she seems to feel that she owns me. ". . .my car."

"One person could own another?"

"Yep."

"And it was always a white person owning a black person?"

"Uh, yes."

"Did you ever own anyone?"

"No, of course not."

"You're white."

"Yes, but this was long, long ago, before I was even born."

"But why was it because of their color?"

"I don't know really. White people came from Europe, black people from Africa, and the white people thought they were superior to the black people."

"Superior? How?"

"You got me."

"We cats know better than that. We're every color of the rainbow. Look at me. How many colors would you say I am?"

I did a quick count. "Six or seven."

"Right, and I'm as good as any cat ."

Sundae thought about this for a moment. "I see black people on television all the time, and they're good at music and sports and politics. You'd better not tangle with old Congressman Lewis, that's for sure."

"Mr. Lincoln once said that he would no more want to own a slave than to be a slave."

"My kind of man."

"Yes, and when he finally got the chance he did all he could to free all of the slaves. Sadly though, he was killed before he got the job completely done."

"Killed?"

"A man who didn't want the slaves freed sneaked up behind him at a theater and shot him in the back of the head."

"A sneak, huh?"

"Yes."

"So Mr. Lincoln, in a way, died for his beliefs."

"That's right."

"A little like Jesus did."

"You might upset some people talking that way."

"He freed the slaves, right, and now everything is hunkey dorrey."

I never cease to be amazed at Sundae's vocabulary. She doesn't read, so far as I know, so she must pick up all her language from television, since she doesn't learn such words from me.

"Not exactly. What you see around you didn't come overnight. It took more than a hundred years after Lincoln died for things to get the way they are."

"Why?"

"The freed slaves were not treated like full citizens. They couldn't vote, they couldn't eat in dining rooms with whites, they couldn't ride in the same railroad cars."

"Pretty sad."

"Yes."

I watched Sundae's face. She was thinking over what I had said. Without looking down at it, she leaned over and took a bite out of the bacon. She chewed it contemplatively. "What changed things?" she asked at last.

"There was a movement for equal rights, just thirty years ago, when I was a teenager, and things began to change. A man named Martin Luther King. . ."

She perked up. "I know him." She lowered her voice. "I've got a dream. . ."

"That's the one."

"Was he a president?"

"No, he was a civil rights leader. We haven't had a black president."

"Still the old feelings?"

"Probably."

"What about Jesse? I see him a lot. People listen to him. Could he be president?"

"Jesse Jackson? I'd like to say it's possible, but how long from now I don't know. By the time people get over their prejudices, Jesse may be too old. But there will be younger black leaders. Maybe one of them will be a president."

"No black president. How about women?"

"No. Not yet."

"All white, all men?"

"Yes, and so far all Christian."

"Christian? Like Jerry Falwell?"

"I mean, no Jewish presidents."

"All white Christian men."

"So far." I thought I would get her opinion about something. We collect human opinions about things all the time, why not feline? I've found that Sundae often has more informed and critical opinions on things than a lot of people do. "Which do you think will come first, a black president, a woman president, or a Jewish president?"

"That's easy," she said. "Jewish."

"Why?"

"Because you humans judge people by their looks. We cats know that you ought to judge people by their souls, not their looks, but you don't. So since a Jew looks just like a Christian, you will have a Jewish president without even knowing it."

"But a Jew is not a Christian."

"Jesus was a Jew, and Christians like him."

"Yes," I admitted.

"Then the next to be president after a Jewish man will be a black man."

"I thought you said we humans judge too much by skin color. Why wouldn't a white woman come before a black man?"

"Because you also judge by sex. I learned that on Oprah. A black man can learn to act, if not look, just like a white man. He can talk and walk and even think the same. A woman, if she is a real woman, Oprah says, wouldn't lower herself to the level of a man."

"You should know, being a woman."

"I am not a woman. I'm a cat."

"Oh yes, that's right."

"You know who will be last to be president? A black woman. She has two strikes against her from the start. And if she were Jewish, strike three!"

I stared at her. She stared at me. I grinned. She grinned back. Then she laughed. It was that great, bellowing laugh she sometimes lets out when she is caught in a big one.

"Would you want to be president, Sundae?" I teased.

"It would never happen," she laughed. "I'm not even human. That's a fourth strike against me. I'm female, partly black, and I feel so kin to Jesus I must be Jewish. Besides, you humans have only had two presidents you really respect in. . .how many years?"

"Two hundred and more. But there have been a few others: Jefferson, F.D.R."

"But you seem to elect screw-ups most of the time. I wouldn't qualify."

We chuckled.

"What about you?" she asked. "Why don't you run for president?"

"No, no. I have the biggest mark of all against me."

"What's that?"

"I'm a teacher."

Sundae really liked that. She went around chuckling the rest of the day.

Sundae is my cat.

APRIL FOOL'S DAY

On the morning of March 31, when I saw there was nothing memorable coming up that day, I flipped my calendar page over to the next month. There at the bottom of the first day's box was the reminder of what day the first of April is. I sat at my desk and started making a list of the various people I felt I knew well enough to pull pranks on the next morning. You have to fool people early on April Fool's Day because after the first hour or so they catch on.

At the bottom of my list I put Sundae's name. I hesitated before adding it because her sense of humor, so totally feline, is hard to predict. As she has adjusted to me, her humor has slowly altered, and she shows evidence of at least understanding what I find funny, if not always why I do. But she fails to laugh at things I find intensely humorous; and she either chuckles or laughs aloud at things that seem to me utterly serious. I was not sure whether an April Fool prank would make any sense to her or not. But I kept her name on the list, thinking that I might as well give it a shot.

That night I looked and saw that her food bowl was getting low, but I did not fill it the way I usually do. After I went to bed, I heard her chewing. She eats mostly dry food, and her eating,with its snap, crackle, and pop, resounds through the house. I knew she was finishing the last of her Friskies. I smiled to myself. Sometime during the night, at the time she has her usual snack, I heard her jump down from her window perch, where she guards me through the dark times, and patter through my bedroom toward her food bowl. I pretended to be asleep. There was a long silence, and then she came back. It was all I could do to keep from laughing. Her footsteps stopped beside my bed. She knows better than to wake me. The only time I have ever shown her my temper is when she pesters me while I sleep. She finally sighed and went back to her perch.

Once more, close to daylight, she jumped down again and went back to her bowl. Maybe she thought I had been up and filled it while she dozed, maybe it was just wishful thinking, but she made another trip. Again she came back and sat near my bed for a long time before heaving an even bigger sigh and going back to the window. I heard her muttering under her breath.

It was a Thursday morning, and I had to go to work, but I took my time waking up. I turned over and yawned three or four times. Each time Sundae jumped down and came over to my bed and waited. Each time I pretended to go back to sleep. Each time she grumbled and went back to the window to watch the sun rising from behind the tall trees across the road.

Finally I got up, but instead of checking on her food, the way I generally do, I went directly into the bathroom, where I took much longer than usual over my ablutions. When I finally came out, Sundae was waiting for me. She had assumed the feline posture that, had she been a human being, would have had her hands on her hips. I could tell by her body language that she was royally miffed.

"What's wrong with you?" I asked innocently.

"Food," she said.

"Food? What about it?"

"I'm out," she said. "If I'm not to get gormet stuff out of a can you could at least make sure I have enough of what I have. I ran out last night. I'm starving."

"You are?" I teased. I was already having a great time. "You look pretty fit to me. Haven't lost any weight that I can tell."

"That's not what I mean. I'm hungry."

"Oh."

I went up to her bowls, one for water, one for food. Sure enough, just as she said, just as I knew, her food bowl was empty.

"You're out of food," I said.

"Yes, I know that," she said disgustedly. "Do you think you might do something about the situation? The sooner the better."

"Maybe I can," I said. I wanted to build her hopes in order to dash them. I'm a pretty mean April Fool player. I take no prisoners. I walked into the kitchen and opened the top door of the cabinet, where I keep Sundae's food. I slowly turned around to face her. She sat in the middle of the floor, expecting service. "There's a problem," I said.

"What?"

"You're out."

"Out?"

"I forgot to shop. You ran out of food yesterday morning, and I intended to stop by for more last night, and I clean forgot it." I laughed self-consciously.

"You forgot. . .my food?" she said. I don't know if you have ever heard the tone a cat's voice displays when she is completely taken aback, but that was Sundae's tone. She was simultaneously surprised, shocked, horrified, and offended. Not pretty.

"Yes, I did. I'm sorry." I let the message sink in deeper. Then I smiled. "But this means we can suffer together. I meant to buy milk for my coffee. You'll go hungry, and I'll have to drink my coffee black." Once more I laughed as if embarrassed.

Sundae's eyes narrowed. "Are you insane?" she said. "You compare hunger, starvation, to coffee without milk?"

"You won't starve," I said. "You can have some of my Fruit Loops." I was really, truly enjoying this.

Sundae huffed and turned around on the spot three times, the way she does before she lies down, except this time she didn't lie down. I waited for her to come unglued, but she just sat there, curled her tail around her legs, and stared at me. This made me nervous.

"I tell you what," I said, "I'll stop by the store on my way home and buy you a new bag, what do you say to that?"

"When will that be?"

"What difference does it make? Cats don't have a sense of time."

"What?"

"I can tell you when I leave that I'll be back in five minutes, and even when I'm gone five hours you don't seem to notice."

"That's because I don't care."

"Oh." That hurt. I had intended to break my joke at this point, but I decided to let the little monster suffer some more, since she did have a sense of time.

"So when will you get back from the store?" she insisted.

"I get out of class at 3:00. I can go by and shop right after that."

I could see the wheels turning in her head. "Three is when Andy and Barney come on," she said. "You mean I have to wait that long?"

"I guess so."

"I could die."

"You won't die. You have a lot of excess fat around your middle. Bottom too."

I saw lightning flash in her eyes. She is very sensitive about her figure. It's easy to offend her by mentioning that she has put on weight.

"I. . .You. . ." she sputtered. It looked like she might be about to explode. I realized I had taken this about as far as possible without having my pajama leg slashed to ribbons.

"April Fool," I said with a laugh.

She just sat there.

"April Fool," I said, more softly.

"What does that mean?" she said.

"I fooled you. I played a trick on you. See?" I threw open the cabinet and pulled a fresh sack of Friskies out and held it up in front of her.

"There's food?" she said. Her voice sounded relieved but yet skeptical.

"Yes. I got a fresh bag last Saturday."

"Then why did you let me think we were out?"

"A trick. A joke. I made you think you would go hungry. I fooled you."

"Why?" She was both angry and puzzled.

"It's April First."

"So?"

"People play tricks on each other on this day."

"Another of your holidays?"

"No. We go to work on this day. If we didn't, we couldn't play tricks."

"Why do you do this? You scared me."

"That's the idea. It's funny." I laughed. She didn't.

"It's funny to trick someone? To scare them? To make them think they might have to go hungry all day and suffer mortal agony? That's funny?"

"Yes. As long as you don't keep it up too long, as long as you tell the person fairly quickly that it's all a joke. Then you laugh, and they laugh, and everyone feels better."

"What if the person doesn't laugh, doesn't find it amusing?"

"Then he's not a good sport."

"Ha!" Sundae said. She was not a good sport and she had no intention of being one.

I shrugged and led her to her bowl. I filled it and left her to eat while I went in to make my coffee, which I actually was able to whiten because I had bought milk along with cat food on Saturday. I could hear her crunching over the gurgle of my coffee maker. She didn't come back into the kitchen even after the crunching had died away, and I assumed she was sulking. I drank my coffee at the kitchen table while I read the morning paper. Then I went into the bathroom to get ready for school. While I was trimming my beard, she came in and jumped up on the edge of the bathtub. I knew she wanted to talk. I waited.

"So you made me an April Fool," she finally said.

"I guess so," I said, trying not to gloat.

"You're smiling," she said.

"Sorry."

"So you do this to a lot of people."

"Yes."

"Do you have any friends left?"

"Of course. They do it to me too."

"Humans!" she huffed.

I began clipping my nostril hairs. She looked at me with disdain. "You humans do some disgusting things. Like the way you go up inside your nose with your scissors. Yah!"

"Much the way you lick yourself all over," I said. "And then in the middle of the night I have to listen to you coughing up your hair balls."

"But I don't try to make other people April Fools."

"Oh no?" I said sarcastically. "You play tricks on me, just the way I did on you, my fine furry friend."

"I do not."

"Yes, you do. You hide as I come to a corner and jump out on me. A couple of times I've dropped what I was carrying because you scared me so badly."

"Well, but that isn't a joke. I'm not trying to make you look silly. I'm not trying to make a Fool out of you."

"What is it if not a joke? What are you trying to do?"

"I'm practicing."

"Practicing? Practicing what?"

"Hunting. I'm keeping in practice. In case I ever have to hunt for my food, I want to be in good shape. Hiding, pouncing, these are necessary to existence in the wild."

"So you're not trying to make me look foolish. You're trying to make me a meal."

"No, I wouldn't eat you. You put too many offensive chemicals on your body. I don't think you would taste very good."

"Thank heaven for that."

"No, my hunting is for practice, to keep me alert, ready to fend for myself."

"You didn't seem ready to fend for yourself this morning when you thought you had run out of Little Friskies."

"That's not funny." She thought about it for a time. " I know, I know, I've become a house cat. Dependent. Soft. I'm not proud of what you've done to me, you know."

"Well, I'm sorry for treating you so well."

"You should be."

"But you play your little games. Your games keep you a cat. They keep you sane. They relieve anxiety about the kind of life you have to lead," I explained patiently. "That's why I play April Fool jokes. They're games. They keep me human by sharpening my mental skills. They relieve anxiety about the kind of life I lead. See?"

She mulled this over for a time. I finished grooming myself and looked in the mirror. It was pretty hopeless, the way I looked in the morning light, but I would have to leave it at that. I would never be young and handsome again. I sighed and went into the bedroom to get dressed. Sundae followed me.

"So you're saying that playing tricks keeps your mind active, like pounching keeps my body active, is that right?"

"Yep."

"Why is it so important to people that they keep their minds active?"

"It's all we've got," I said. I sat down to put on my socks and shoes. "Humans would not have survived in the jungles at the beginning of our history, let alone have risen to the top, without our minds. We're not the strongest animals. Lots of them could have killed us. We're not the fastest, nor the best tree climbers, nor the best swimmers. We can't fly or run very fast or fight very well in hand to hand combat with other animals. So we survived by our wits, we made tools to fight with, and finally we conquered all the others because we were the smartest."

"That might be a matter of controversy," Sundae said.

"You depend on me for your livelihood. That shows who won."

"Maybe. Or maybe I see you as my servant."

That did indeed make some sense. I had often thought about how I went to work every day while Sundae lounged at home. I put food in her bowl and cleaned her litter box. Maybe cats were the smartest of creatures. Maybe we humans were born to labor for them.

"But I still don't see why you couldn't exercise your minds in a different way," she went on. Why couldn't you play games that aren't cruel?"

"Do you think April Fool jokes are cruel?"

"They certainly are."

I finished putting on my shoes and went back into the kitchen to get the sandwich I had put together the night before for my lunch. Sundae followed me. As I packed my bag with the sandwich, chips, and a drink, she jumped up on the counter. Usually I discourage her from getting up there, but this time I didn't because it put her on my eye level. The teacher in me needed to look my pupil in the pupil.

"Maybe the April Fool joke reveals human nature at its truest," I said, eye to eye with her. "Maybe we need to keep our wits sharp by being cruel. After all, it's always been, and it still is, a dog-eat-dog world."

"Pew-ee," Sundae said. I didn't know whether she was put off by the truth of human personality or by the canine figure of speech. I just nodded in agreement. "You got it, kid."

I turned to go and get my coat, and as I left the room I heard Sundae jump down. Then I heard a groan followed by a yowl. I turned back and saw her rolling on the floor.

"Sundae!" I said. "What is it?"

"Ooohhh," she said. "Ooohhh, the pain."

I put down my bag and rushed over to her. She lay on her side, looking down at her right hind leg. "What did you do?" I asked.

"I came down wrong on it," she moaned. She got to her paws and tried to walk, but she had to favor that leg, and every time she put weight on it she let out a cry of pain.

I panicked. She had never hurt herself before. She had suffered through a couple of colds and small illnesses, but she had never been injured. "Oh, Sundae," I said in sympathy. I picked her up as gently as I could, rushed out to the car with her in my arms, made her comfortable in the seat beside me, and drove at breakneck speed to the Vet's office. Fortunately he was already at work, and I fast-talked Sundae and myself past a large managerie of dogs and cats into his office. I tried to explain to him what had happened, but I was too excited to be very articulate, so finally I just stood aside to let him work on my precious little pet.

An hour and a hundred dollars later, after an x-ray of the paw and a precautionary shot to relax her, the Vet told me that from all he could tell, there was nothing wrong with her. I wanted to argue, to tell him how much she had suffered, but I hated to tell him he was wrong. He gave me some pain formula and told me to bring her back if she seemed still to be suffering the next day. Cats sprain legs all the time, he said a bit callously I thought, and she would recover. Not to worry, he reassured me.

Reluctantly I paid the bill and took her home, driving slowly this time to avoid bumps that might hurt her more, thinking all the time about how brave she had been. She had not made any verbal complaint throughout her ordeal.

I carried her to her bed and put her in it. I went to her litter box and tidied it up. I put more Friskies in her bowl. I went back to her. "I hate to leave you, Sundae," I said sincerely. "I have to go to class. But right after my class I'll come back and spend the lunch hour here." I usually didn't return until my afternoon classes were over, but my darling was hurt. "Will you be all right?"

"I think so," she sighed.

"At least there wasn't a break."

"No," she said.

"Are you in pain?"

"The shot helped."

"Good." I patted her on the head and lingered to give her ears a gentle scratching. Then I went to get my brief case and sandwich bag. As I was collecting my gear I heard her jump down from her perch. I listened as her footsteps came across the floor. I watched in amazement as she came through the door to the room where I was standing. She wasn't limping.

"Sundae!" I said, amazed at her coordination.

"Yes?" she said, smiling.

"You're not limping."

"No."

"Why not?"

"I've been sharpening my wits, acting human."

"What?"

"April Fool!"

Sundae is my cat.

EASTER

The long, cold, dreary season passed at last. It seemed like an eternity since October had ended the warm weather and we had been plunged into the state of depression called winter.

I had almost despaired of seeing extended sunny times again when, one morning in late March, the dark clouds thinned, the sun peeped through, and my heart started to believe things might get better, that spring would come.

I'm not sure how affected Sundae is by weather. She never goes outside, so in her tightly controlled and protected world the temperature is always the same. She seemed to feel more energetic, less irritable as the spring weather set in; but that may have just been because I felt better, treated her better, brought out the better nature in her. We both were easier to live with as April came.

One Sunday morning, I was reading the paper. My third cup of coffee was beside me. Sundae sat in a window facing out onto the front porch, sunning herself. I was deep into a story about prostate surgery, something all men my age read about with fear and trepidation, when I saw her, out of the corner of my eye, suddenly stand up.

"Whoa!" she said.

"What's the matter?"

Her legs were stiff, and her tail was bushy. I always know she's in a state of alert when she stands that way with a puffy tail.

"Come look what some bird did."

I was accustomed to seeing a lot of bird poop on my porch. How they do it I don't know. There's no place for them to perch. They must dive bomb me. I was ready for a major splash to clean up, but that wasn't what Sundae meant. Near my front door was a small blue basket, with a big red bow, and inside it three brightly multicolored Easter eggs.

"Oh," I chuckled. "How nice."

"Nice? Why can't they lay those things in trees? Don't they know some dog will come along and eat their babies?"

"Sundae!" I feigned exasperation. "A bird didn't leave those eggs. A neighbor did. Probably that cute little girl across the street. Meg."

"Meg lays eggs?"

"No, her mother probably did them for me."

"Her mother lays eggs?"

I looked at Sundae with a cocked eye. It's sometimes hard to tell what she does and does not know. I was pretty sure she really did at first think a bird had left the eggs; but I was also pretty sure that she understood before that last question that Meg's mother did not lay eggs.

"Those are boiled eggs, Sundae. They're colored like that after they're boiled. They're Easter eggs. Let's get them inside. You may be right about the dog."

I went to the porch and brought the tiny basket inside and put it gently on my breakfast table. Sundae soon joined me. I picked up each egg in turn and looked at the elaborate designs. Sundae watched me. I knew we were about to have a philosophical discussion.

"Easter, huh?" she said. "So, you gonna tell me about it or not?"

"Well", I said, "it's a religious holiday, in the spring like now, when Christians celebrate the resurrection of Jesus."

"Resurrection?"

"Rising from the dead."

Now she cocked an eye at me. "He. . .what?"

"Yes. Believers say that on Sunday after he was crucified he

63

rose from the dead and appeared to his followers. That's why he's considered divine."

"He died for his ideas, like Lincoln, right?"

"Right."

"Did Lincoln rise from the dead?"

"No."

"But Elvis did."

"Sundae! Where did you hear that?"

"Believe It Or Not. They say someone saw him eating in a Burger King in Paris, Texas, last July 21. Believe It Or Not."

She was smiling.

"I believe it not."

"You have no sense of humor."

"Anyway, do you like my eggs?"

"Pretty," she said. "Why eggs?"

"Lots of reasons," I said, trying to gather my memories. I had read several explanations for this symbol. "Some people say the chick coming out of the egg is like Jesus coming out of his tomb. In the Greek Orthodox Church people go around on Easter knocking each other's eggs together, to see which one breaks first."

"Messy."

"Yes. But here we hard boil them."

"So no chicks are about to come out of these."

"That's true."

"So the symbol is lost."

"True again. But about the meaning, I guess since Easter comes in the spring, the whole holiday symbolizes resurrection. Notice how the trees and flowers are budding out there?"

She looked through the window. "I notice."

"Well, flowers, trees, birds, bees, rabbits laying eggs..."

"Rabbits laying eggs?"

"All right. That's a myth. It's only birds that lay eggs, right?"

"No. Fish do. Alligators do. I've watched Wild Kingdom. But rabbits, no sir, I don't believe they do." She sounded playful.

"Right again. But Easter brings out all the symbols of new life, the world reborn, resurrected after the dead winter, and reminds us that there is hope."

"But why rabbits?"

"I guess because they are so prolific. You know, they have so many babies. And especially in the spring, you see them everywhere."

"I've noticed. Especially on the Playboy Channel."

Sundae watches a lot of television. I guess she's bored when I'm away at school. Her taste is, shall we say, eclectic. But it surprised me just a bit that she would watch the Playboy Channel. After all, she's a cat, and she's a girl, and she is spayed.

"What have you seen on the Playboy Channel?"

"Bunnies. Lots of bunnies. Not the kind that run around in your yard. These are women dressed in bathing suits, with rabbit ears and tails. Heff calls them his bunnies."

"Heff? So you know Hugh Heffner."

"I don't exactly know him. He's not one of your friends, and remember, the only humans I meet are friends of yours. He's never been here, right?"

"Right. But you seem to know him well enough to call him Heff."

"That's what the bunnies call him."

"Those are bunnies of a different kind."

She thought over what we had said for a time. I always enjoy watching her think, those wheels turning in there. Finally she seemed satisfied that she had it straight—so far. Now she was ready to go on. "So is Easter like the other holidays?" she said..

"Well, it's unique, it has its own character."

"What strange things do people do on Easter?"

"Well, they often buy new clothes to wear."

"Why?"

"I guess it's the right time to buy new spring clothes. And it's a symbol of bringing in a new life, a new season, taking on a new appearance. People like to dress up in their new clothes and go to church."

"This has to do with Jesus, right?"

"Yes. Lots of people I know only go to church twice a year, Easter and Christmas."

"Why do people go to church any time?"

"To. . .be. . .closer to God, I suppose."

"So some of them only need to be closer to God twice a year?"

"Seems that way. But I guess they feel they want to go on those two days. They're the most holy of all."

"Most holy. What does holy mean?"

"Sacred." That didn't explain it. "Close to God."

"Why are certain days holier than others? And come to think of it, why do you have to go to church to be close to God?"

"People seem to need to set aside certain times and places and spaces and make them special. They like to go to church at a specific time and feel they are sure God is there."

"But isn't God everywhere, all the time?"

"Yes."

"Humans!" Sundae said with that mixture of amazement and frustration. "So people go to church on Easter, when they might not go any other time."

"Except Christmas."

"Yes, yes."

"On Easter they remember the resurrection of Jesus, from way back on that Sunday morning when his followers first found his tomb empty."

"Empty tomb? So they just guessed he came back from the dead."

"At first. Then some of them said they saw him."

"This was on a Sunday morning."

"Yes. In fact, this Easter there will be a sunrise service out by the city lake. People will get up before daybreak and go out and have a service when the sun comes up."

"Now that's dedication."

Sundae, oddly for a cat, likes to sleep late. Some cats get up before their human companions. Some even wake their humans up. But Sundae likes her rest, day and night. She is maybe the laziest creature I have ever known. I would never tell her that, of course, but it's true.

"A couple of places people put on a play and act out the events of the first Easter. There's some place in Austria, I think, where they do it, all out in the open, and Jesus comes back from the dead and talks with his friends."

"I'd like to see that. Can we go?"

"It might be hard. You would have to stay in quarantine if I took you to a foreign country. They're afraid animals carry disease."

"And humans don't?"

"No, we do too."

"Sheer bigotry then."

"What do you expect from us humans?"

She ignored my sarcasm. "This resurrection thing. It's really important to you, isn't it? Is that because Jesus had died young?"

"I guess so, in part."

"So rising from the dead gave him a chance to live out the rest of his life, until he was an old man, like you."

"Not really. He didn't hang around very long. He went on up to live in heaven after just a few days."

"Wasn't that where he already was?"

"Probably."

"Then why come back? Just to say a proper goodbye?"

"Maybe to tell people there's life after death?" I was reaching. I'm no theologian. I'm not even a philosopher. And I have to admit I go to church usually only twice a year. "Life after death?" She cocked her head at me. "You believe you're gonna rise from the dead too, like Jesus?"

"I plead ignorance. I may."

"Just to say a proper goodbye to your friends?"

I laughed. Sundae sometimes jumps to conclusions. "No, I don't mean I'll rise from the dead and walk around. But maybe I'll have some kind of life after this one."

"What kind?"

"Well, there's a lot of disagreement about that. Some people say there's nothing beyond death, just stillness, quiet, your spirit passes away with your body; you live on, if at all, in other people's memories."

"Makes sense to me," Sundae said thoughtfully.

"Other people believe you will just be reabsorbed into the Great Being of Life, that you're like a drop of water that comes out of a lake for a time and then goes back into the lake."

"Yes," Sundae said. The wheels in her head were turning. "Go on."

"Some people believe you come back to this earth in another form. Maybe another animal."

"What? They believe that after I die I'll come back as another animal? Which one?"

"They say it depends on how good you were at being what you were in this life. If you were the best cat you could be, you might come back. . ." I knew I was in quicksand here.

"Yes? Come back as what? You weren't going to say as a dog."

"No."

"Not a horse or something like that."

"No."

"Don't tell me, you were going to say I could, if I acted just as good as possible while a cat, I might come back as a. . .human." I hung my head and looked at her with a crooked smile. "You were! You were going to say that, weren't you? I knew it. That old human bias. Just because you run the world you think you're what every creature wants to be. Boy, do you people have a nerve. I FOR ONE would not want to be a human under any circumstances."

"Yes, I know."

"What do you think? About life after death."

"I really don't know what's gonna happen. When I was growing up, I was taught that I would live on after death and that I would still be me. So I should try to improve myself and be the best me it's possible to be."

"Where would you live then? Here?"

"No. I was taught that the place was called Heaven."

"Heaven. Sounds nice. Just you?"

"No. My family. My friends. Lots of other people."

"Lots of other people? What about cats?"

"Uh, I don't think so. It was never mentioned."

"Not dogs."

"No. Nor horses, nor deer. It's odd, I'd never thought of it before, but in the Heaven we were taught there weren't any animals at all. Just us humans. . .and God."

"No animals? You're an animal."

"Well, sort of."

"Sort of?" Sundae stood up and bowed her back. "You're special?"

"That's what we were taught. Man at the top, and all the other animals in a separate category. Well, categories. Next to us were animals friendly to us, then ones who served us, and then the ones who would harm us unless we got to them first."

"Dogs are in that lowest category, aren't they?"

"Some are."

"So, the rest of us were not in your Heaven, right? What was supposed to happen to us when we died?"

"I don't know."

"Were we like those drops of lake water? Did we keep going up and down in the animal world forever? Was there a Cat Heaven?"

"Maybe. I've only heard of one other animal with its own Heaven."

"Don't tell me."

"Yes. Dogs."

Sundae began to sway her striped tail about. I could tell the conversation was at an end. She jumped down from the chair and walked away.

"See you on Easter," she said.

I didn't know whether she planned to hide from me for the next week, or if this was a threat that she would challenge me to see who had a life after this one. With Sundae you never know.

Sundae is my cat.

MEMORIAL DAY

I seldom take Sundae for rides in the car. After that first Christmas, which she later told me was "hell" for her, I promised her that I would never again take her for a long drive, that if I had to make one of those "death march" trips, I would leave her at home and have a friend come in to feed and care for her. So she now goes out only to see the Vet—or when I want her to see something special.

I never tell my friends and colleagues that she can talk because they would think I'm crazy and out of pity and concern probably lock me up—for my own good. Sundae is careful never to say anything when I have guests because I have warned her that if she does, she might end up in the circus among the freaks. Only once did she slip and say something, and fortunately for both of us my guest that night had drunk so much wine that she thought she just imagined it, and we were able later to laugh away what we called her hallucination.

Because Sundae can talk and discuss things with me in a more intelligent way than most of my human friends, I decided one bright, sunny afternoon in late May to put her in the car with me and take her to see something special. I didn't warn her in advance because if she knows her routine is going to be altered, even the slightest bit, she becomes insomniac. Not only does she stay up and wander through the house all night before we go, she keeps me up too. That day after lunch, without warning, I scooped her up and took her, amid vocal protests, and dumped her in the front seat of the car. Another thing I had promised her was that I would never again put her in a carrying cage. Besides, the whole purpose of the trip was for her to see something new, and she couldn't see out from a cage.

She groused for a few minutes, as I backed out of my drive-

71

way and started up the street; but before long she was absorbed in the scenery and fell silent. She so seldom got out of our house that everything she saw was a novelty for her. We didn't talk much as I drove, not until I slowed down, took a right, and pulled into the cemetery. Then at last she spoke.

"What is this?" she asked. Her voice had an ominous tone, as though the neatly trimmed grass and white tombstones spoke some somber, threatening message to her.

"It's a graveyard," I said. I sometimes surprise myself when I use old fashioned words like that. I think it happens when I refer to something that I recall from my earliest childhood, when the "older generation" used terms that are now antiquated.

"Graveyard?"

"Cemetery," I used the modern term. "It's where they bury people."

"Dead people?"   She drew back from the window.

"They wouldn't bury people still alive," I said, trying to be funny. Sundae didn't laugh. She seldom laughs at my jokes.

"What are the rocks?"

"They're markers. Can you see the writing on them?"

"She leaned her front paws against the glass and peered out. "Yes."

"That tells you who is buried there and when they lived."

"Some of them have pictures."

"Yes."

"Lots of them have flowers."

"Yes."

"And there are flags."

"Yes. People leave flowers to say they love the person buried there. The flags, though, are only on the graves of veterans."

"What?"

I knew I would have to explain it, but we had come to the place for me to stop, so I waited until I had turned off my engine. Then I scooped Sundae up and carried her in my arms out to the place where my mother and father are buried. I still didn't trust her to walk around on her own outside. I had placed flowers on my parents' graves just the month before, and since I always buy silk ones they still looked fresh. I balanced Sundae, who I noticed had gained weight, on one arm and pulled a small silk flag out of my side pocket. Then I leaned over and planted it above my dad's headstone.

"What is this all about?" Sundae said. She sat upright in the crook of my arm.

"It's Memorial Day," I said. "That's what all the flags are for. They are to remember people who died in wars."

"Died in wars?" she said. "You mean from gunshots? Or bombs or tank fire? Like on The War Channel?"

"You watch War a lot, don't you?" I said.

"When I can't find a Jerry or Oprah."

"Yes, well, that's how most veterans who die die. That's how my dad died. See the dates on the two stones?"

"I can't read, remember?" Sundae said.

"Okay, look then. Here's my mother's dates. See? It says under her name 1928—1992. She lived to be 64, which is a normal life span for a human." I saw Sundae's eyebrows begin to rise, as they always do when she is about to ask a question, but I hurried on because I didn't want to get into the injustice of a cat's brevity. "Now this is my father. See? Under his name it says 1927—1951. That's not a normal lifespan. He died when he wasn't quite 24."

"How?"

"In combat. Like on The War Channel. He was shot."

"How old were you then?"

"Zero."

"Zero? How could you be zero?"

"I wasn't born. I came along six months after he died."

"Which war was it? The Revolutionary War, The War of 1812, The Civil War, The Great War, or World War Two, or Korea, or Vietnam?"

I was impressed. "You've sure learned a lot from The War Channel," I said.

"I guess I have. But I also have a family interest." I started to ask her to explain that cryptic remark, but she quickly said, "Which war killed your father?"

"Korea," I said. "He was one of those men called up on Monday and dead on Saturday."

"What?"

"Just a figure of speech. The army called up thousands of boys late in 1950, and they went into battle before they were trained properly, and they mostly all got killed."

"Pretty dumb."

"Yes." I rubbed my cheek against my shoulder. "Pretty dumb all right."

"Why are you doing that?" Sundae looked up to my face.

"What?"

"Water is dribbling out of your eyes."

"Guess I'm crying."

"Crying? What is that? I've seen people on Oprah do that. Never on The War Channel, I notice, but other places. I've never seen you do it. What is it?"

"Humans do it when they're sad. I'm sad thinking about my father. He never saw me. In fact, I don't think he ever knew about me."

"Your mother never told him?"

"I must have happened just as he was leaving. By the time she knew, he was on the front lines, and by the time a letter about me would have arrived, he was dead. Mother said several of her letters to him were returned unopened. She never exactly said the first news about me was in one of them, but I think she was just sparing my feelings."

"That is sad," Sundae said. And then she did something really odd. She leaned up and rubbed her nose against mine. I say odd because cats do not to my knowledge cry, and they really don't understand when humans do. Some of them seem to know something is wrong when humans cry, and I have heard of cats jumping up into a mourner's lap and embracing him or her to stop the outpouring of grief. Now Sundae is not that demonstrative—or that sympathetic. While she will sometimes rub against my leg and will tolerate it when I sometimes rub noses with her, she had never before done it to me. This was the closest she had ever come to giving me a kiss. It was by far her greatest show of affection or sympathy ever.

I had had enough of sadness for one day, so I walked back to the car and pitched her in. I cranked up and drove all through the cemetery, looking at the brightly and patriotically decorated graves. Sundae watched the scene through her glass. She was quiet until we got back out onto the road. It was as if she wanted to show respect by keeping silent. Only as we returned home did she speak.

"It's a nice thing, what you did, what the others have done," she said. "If a person has to die, it's good at least to have a stone. And I like the flags."

"Me too."

"So many cats die under bridges and are never remembered."

"Yes, I know."

"You will always go there on this day, to remember your dad, won't you?"

"Yes. But I don't know whether my daughter will or not. Memory in humans usually lasts only about a generation."

"Cats remember much longer."

"Do they?"

"Oh yes. I know all about my ancestors, back to fifty generations."

"How did you learn about them?"

"I absorbed it, through my mother's milk."

"Do cats have collective memory?"

"What's that?"

"Are you born with the memories of your race?"

"No. We have to be taught. My mother taught me, before I was weaned."

"Where did your ancestors come from?"

"Virginia. One of my great, great, grands was the first person to welcome General Robert E. Lee back from the Civil War, my mother said." So it wasn't just through The War Channel that Sundae knew her history. She had a family history as well, and anyone's family history must take into consideration our many wars. "The general's first act after returning home, Mother said, was to fill my great, great grand's bowl with fresh sweet milk."

"Milk isn't good for a cat, you know that."

"I know. Still, it was a nice gesture."

"I guess. You know, it was the Civil War that got Memorial Day started." I was moving back into my teacher role. Fortunately, I have an inquisitive cat, else I would probably bore her to death. Instead of yawning, she perked up. That encouraged me to go on. "In 1868, just three years after the war ended, women began going to the graves of their dead husbands and fathers and decorating them with flowers and flags."

"Only women?"

"In most of our wars, men die and women mourn."

"I resent that. I know it's true, but I resent it. Females can fight, and men can mourn."

"Yes. And in the future there may be more of both."

She cocked her head and started to ask why that would be true, but then she seemed to think better of it. "Go on," she said.

"Well, at first this happened only in the north, in the states that were loyal to the Union during the war. Southern women may have done it, but they did it any day they wished. Only in the northern states was it an official day. They called it Decoration Day. That was true until the end of World War I, the one you call The Great War. In 1919 Congress declared May 30 a Memorial Day for all war dead."

"So then everyone was honored."

"Yes. Except some southern states voted not to have it on the national day. Different ones have it different days."

"Why? Aren't southerners good Americans?"

"Yes. They've died in all the American wars since. In fact, most southerners, oddly enough, think they're better Americans than Yankees. But southerners, well, they like to be different."

"What was that business this morning on television? Billy Clinton carried a big wreath up to a monument and put it down and looked sad for several seconds."

"You saw that?"

"Yes. While you were asleep."

"Oh. Well, yes, that was at the Tomb of the Unknown Solider. The president always goes there and lays a wreath."

"I like Billy Clinton, even when he looks so sad, especially when he looks sad. He always looks like a little boy who's done something naughty."

"Sometimes it's true," I said.

"Yes," she sighed. "But back to the point, where is this Tomb?"

"Arlington."

"Arlington? That was where my ancestor lived with General Lee."

"That's right. Arlington was a big plantation. Lee came to be master of it through his marriage. During the war, since it was so close to Washington, since Lee led the Rebels, the Union army decided to bury its war dead on his property so that he could never farm it again."

"Naughty. Naughtier than anything poor Billy Clinton ever did."

"Are you a southern sympathizer, Sundae?"

"General Lee treated us pretty well."

"I see."

"Real men like cats. Sissies like dogs. I think General Grant had a dog."

"Probably. I think they both had horses."

"Well, didn't everyone?"

"I think so."

"Everybody still does."

"I don't."

"Yes you do. You call this car a Mustang. It has a horse on the side of it."

It was Sundae's idea of a joke. I looked at her, and she grinned.

"Yes," I laughed.

She seemed pleased that she had cheered me up, and she turned to look out the window the rest of the way home. When we got there, I carried her inside, and she went for a long late lunch.

After a while she came to the screened-in back porch where I was reading. "You ever go to war?" she asked me as she took a seat on the chair opposite me.

"No," I admitted.

"Why not? You humans have had one every few years. Surely one came along when you were still physically fit."

"Thank you," I said and grinned at her, but she just stared at me, waiting for an answer. "Yes, one came along when I was fit. Vietnam."

"You didn't go?"

"No."

"Why not? Afraid to die like your father?"

"Probably. I used other excuses. I used the fact that I was married, a father, and a graduate student to avoid going."

"A man on Oprah said he had 'conscientious objection' to Vietnam. You too?"

"It's funny. I don't really know. I never went out and protested. I didn't go and fight. I guess I'm just not very ideological, Sundae."

"What does that mean? Ideological. You don't have guts?"

"That's what some people would say. Some on both sides. I didn't try to stop the war, I didn't fight it."

"The man on Oprah said he thought men who went to Vietnam were war criminals. Then there was the other man, the one who tried to slug him. He called the first guy a communist."

"I knew all the arguments. I just didn't buy any of them. Men in my family have been dying in wars for centuries. The generals all get to come home and pet the cat, while my kind get blown to bits. I guess I just didn't want that to happen to me. I wanted to stay home and pet my cat and be left alone."

"So all you can do on Memorial Day is remember your dad and cry."

"And remember a lot of other men who died." I thought about it for a minute. " Sundae, I've never told anyone this before, but I'm gonna tell you."She perked up again. Rubbing noses didn't much turn her on, but sharing confidences did. I could tell I had her attention. "At the start of each semester," I said, "they send me a list of students in my classes who are receiving Veterans' Benefits. I'm supposed to make sure they all come to class and do their work. Well, one term the name of a pretty little blond girl appeared on my list, and I asked her after class if she were a veteran. She said no, and I said, 'Your name is on the list of people receiving aid,' and she said, 'Oh, that's because my father was killed in Vietnam.' I was floored. She was the age to be my own daughter, and I was probably the age of her father. He had gone and been killed and would never know her, while I had stayed home and survived. Well, she wasn't a particularly good student, but believe me, I made sure she got a good grade."

"You cheated for her?"

"Let's say I stretched the rules a bit."

"Why?"

"Maybe I saw my daughter in her. Maybe I saw myself in her father."

"Maybe you felt guilty because he died and you didn't."

"May be."

Sundae thought about what I had said. "You're a good man, James," she finally said. "Better than most, I'd say. You may not have guts, but you got a lotta heart."

We sat for a long time in silence, with Sundae flipping her tail from side to side above her head. I knew she was mulling over all we had talked about. Everything I tell her goes into that great, swirling mix master in her brain. After maybe a half hour, after I had gone back to my reading, she spoke.

"You humans could learn a thing or two from us cats."

"I'm sure of it."

"Don't be flippant. We could teach you a lot about war and peace."

"Well, you are the ones we come home to, if we survive."

"That's right. We do things that avoid war."

"Like. . ."

"We stay clear of each other, except to mate and for nourishment as kittens."

"I've noticed you don't seem to like each other much. You and those cats that comes up on our porch yowl at each other like mortal enemies."

"Yes, but that is better than fighting. We may yowl, but we don't fight like dogs do, where the chances of injury are so great, and we never organize into armies, like you humans, where the chances of dying are so great."

"True."

"We each mark out a small territory, not a great land, to call our own. We can protect it without having to die. We have no reason to go to war. You could learn a lot."

"From the cat?"

"From the cat."

I had to agree. Sundae is my cat.

THE FOURTH OF JULY

Summers are quiet in my town. Perhaps too quiet. Without the college, my town would have no reason to exist. When the spring term ends, the town almost shuts down.

It's dead over the Christmas break, from about mid-December to mid-January, and then again during June, July, and August. I could walk stark naked down my street, or over across the campus, during those two periods, and no one would see me.

I shouldn't forget the few thousand souls who live here year round, but they are mostly older people who are quiet all the time. They tend to go south in the winter and to the mountains in the summer. But even when the local citizens are here, it's the college kids who make all the noise, driving by my house all night, playing their car stereos so high the bass notes rattle my windows, shouting at each other as if having to sit through classes has dammed up so much energy they either have to yell it out or pop. When they're gone, my town gets really still.

I remember Sundae's first full summer with me. By June the students were gone, and with the windows open to let in the warm breezes, she grew accustomed to the town's summer peace and quiet. The quiet came slowly, with students drifting away a handful at a time over several days, and by July she was firmly adjusted to deep, long-lasting, uninterrupted tranquility.

That's probably why it was such a shock to her, at sundown on July 4, to hear the fireworks go off over at the football stadium. There was no warning, not if you can't read the newspapers. All of a sudden there came a whirring, then piercing, then swooping rocket sound, followed by an explosion that felt like it shook the foundations of my house. Sundae was crossing the room, heading over to get a bite to eat as she does every forty-five minutes all day and night, when the first sound reached us. She stopped dead, and every hair on her back stood up as the rocket lifted higher and higher, then fell to her back with the explosion. Her legs bent as she looked all around the ceiling; and before she could take a step there came a second swoop and boom, this one louder than the first. Again her hair rose and fell, and this time instead of looking at the ceiling, she looked at me. By the end of the third attack, she was in my lap.

Sundae isn't a touchy-feeley kind of cat. On rare occasions she lets me pet her, and on cold nights she will jump up and sit in my lap while I read or watch television. But there is always something to be gained by her intimacy, some kind of physical stimulation or comfort. She never comes close to me out of any sense of comradeship. This was not comradeship either, it was fear. I realized that she had probably not had anything else to fear since coming to live at my house, the lucky little devil.

For a good fifteen minutes the swooshing and booming continued, and for that whole time Sundae kept her head buried under my arm. I just laughed and patted her rather large bottom and held her close, trying to let her know that I wasn't afraid and that she shouldn't be either. It was not until there was a lull in the noise, and Sundae thought it was over, that she raised her head and looked into my eyes.

"James, what in the hell was that?" she moaned.

I had never heard her speak with that tone of voice. She is usually upbeat and confident. I could hear the deep imprint of terror in her wavering words.

"It was just fireworks," I told her.

"Fireworks? It sounded like rockets and bombs."

"I know it sounds that way, but it's just noise. It can't hurt you." Then I thought about what I had said. "It can't hurt you unless you get too close to it. The men shoot the fireworks off into the sky, not at people."

"It sounded like a war."

"Well, you should be used to that. You watch The War Channel."

I try to joke with Sundae, but she usually ignores my humor. Either she doesn't catch it or she finds it crude.

"The War Channel's different. I know it's just a story. Besides, I keep the volume low on it. It's far away. That sounded like it was right up the street."

"It was. They do it over at the football field."

"Is that why it shook the earth?"

"Yes. Sound does that."

"I'm glad it's over."

Just then it started again. I guess the men who set the fireworks off had stopped for a smoke, or they had reached the end of one row and it took them a minute or two to start another. Anyway, without warning, the noise hit us again. Sundae was sitting in my lap, facing me, when we got the second round. She literally dived into the space between my hip and the arm of the easy chair and tried to burrow out of sight. She might have succeeded if she had not put on so much weight. But she stayed that way, trembling, her ample bottom on display, as the second wave broke over us. It seemed to last longer than the first. When it ended, I could smell burning powder, even though I live probably a half mile from the field. Sundae waited a long time before she came out of hiding and faced me again.

"Will it never end?" she said.

"Sure it will. We live in a small town. We can't afford to buy enough fire power to go on and on through the night," I assured her.

"Will there be another one?"

"I don't know. I doubt it. I imagine they will have the speeches now."

Just then I heard the faint echo of an amplified voice. I couldn't understand the words, but I felt sure this marked the beginning of the second phase of the program. "I think you're safe."

She sighed and shook herself, as if to shed her fear and her embarrassment at being afraid.Sundae has a lot of pride.

"Speeches? What speeches?"

"Well, on this night, after the fireworks, people get up and talk. It's an old tradition. They tell everyone how lucky we are to be Americans."

"What is all this? They make noises like a Napoleonic battle, and then they make speeches about America?"

"Yes."

"Why?"

"It's the Fourth of July."

"Yes? So? Yesterday was the Third, and tomorrow will be the Fifth. Why is the Fourth so blessed special?"

"You've never heard about the Fourth of July?"

"No."

"Ever heard about July Fourteenth in France?"

"No. None of my ancestors came from France."

"Did you ever hear about Thomas Jefferson?"

"Of Virginia? Yes, of course. One of my great, great grands belonged to him. One of the females from his family was given to a little boy in the Lee family, and that's how we got to Arlington. Some of us stayed at Montecello, but not the ones that I came from."

"What do you know about Mr. Jefferson?"

"I know he liked cats, so he must have been a gentleman. He invented the litter box, did you know that?"

"I knew he was an inventor. I've seen pictures of the bed he made. It fit into the wall between two rooms, so he could get up into his library on one side and into his sitting room on the other. Really clever."

"Yes. But his greatest invention was the litter box. It was when he was old. He got tired of getting up in the night to let my great, great grandfather out; so he ground up some clay into fine grains and mixed it with Eucalyptis leaves, and taught him to use it at night. Then he emptied it out every few days. He saved the lives of a lot of cats that way. After that we didn't have to go outside during the night and cross the porch where the dogs slept."

"A nice man."

"Brilliant."

"Well, anyway, on this day in 1776, people signed Jefferson's Declaration of Independence in Philadelphia, and that is why we make noise and speeches."

"Independence? From what?"

"England. England owned us then, and a group of men wanted us to be independent, so at their meeting they gave Jefferson the job of writing down how they felt."

"How did they feel?"

"Mad."

"Why?"

"The Americans felt like they were grownups and that England was still treating them as if they were children."

"I guess that time comes in every family, doesn't it?"

"Yes. How do you know?"

"Oprah had a show about it. Mothers and daughters. Fathers and sons. The old ones think the young ones are babies; and the young ones think they're grown up. Oprah showed us that it's no one's fault. It's just. . .human."

Sundae said "human" with some sarcasm. I chose to let it pass. For a being who depends on a "human" for food and shelter, she can be strangely caustic on the subject of humanness.

"Well, anyway, on this day, the Americans declared that they were independent, and thus this is Independence Day, and what you've been hearing is celebration."

"So you say that now they are making speeches?"

"Listen."

We sat there in the quietness, our ears still ringing from the fireworks, and by straining we could make out the faint echo of words. They were elevated and stilted, public address rather than conversation, obviously beamed out to the distance with electronic amplification.

"And is the bombing over?"

"Yes."

"Can we go?"

"Go? Where? To the speeches?"

"Yes. I'm an American. I deserve to be included in the festivities, don't I?"

"You'll have to get in your cage."

Sundae huffed. "Why?" She still considered the cage an insult.

"There might be dogs."

"Can't you drive?"

I hadn't thought of that. I always walk when I go to the football field to watch a game or on occasion to jog. "Sure, I guess," I admitted. "Are you ready?"

"Yes. I licked myself all over this afternoon."

So I picked her up and took her to the car, and we drove the short distance to the big parking lot by the stadium, where the fireworks and speeches were being offered to the people of our fair city who were not on vacation. I was lucky to see a car pull out of a spot near the speaker's platform, someone I suppose who had come for the fireworks and wasn't interested in speeches, so I was able to park close enough for us to stay in the car and hear the speakers.

Sundae eased up and peeked over the dash board, through the window, and when she was sure no one could see her, she gazed out at the lights and colorful banners and at the men up on the stage telling us how lucky we were to be citizens of the U. S. of A. I got tired of the whole business very quickly, but to my amazement Sundae drank it all in for the whole hour. Several times I hinted that we might go, but each time she shushed me and kept her ears open to hear more. She even wanted to listen to the Gospel Quartet sing some pretty awful patriotic hymns before it was finally obvious the program was ending and she consented to let me make a getaway before we got caught in the departing traffic. I have a phobia about that. I have to be the first car out of a parking lot.

Sundae was quiet as we drove the short distance home. I carried her inside, and she had a quick snack before she came in to talk with me about the event.

"Interesting, James," she began. "So the Yanks won, did they?"

"I guess so. We got our independence."

"I use Yanks as a general term. A Yank then was both southern and northern, right?"

"Yes."

"Because, didn't you hear, one of the Yanks was Lighthorse Harry Lee from Virginia. He was the man Mr. Jefferson sent my great, great grand home with, for his little daughter. And you know who that girl's youngest brother was, don't you? Robert, who was met when he came home from Appomattox by that great, great grand's great, great, great grandson. We were important to the Lee's, very important."

"I can see."

"So we really kicked some English butt."

"Well, at least we outlasted them. I think they just got tired. They had a lot better equipment than we did, but they were a long way from home, and by keeping the war going so long, we wore them down, dissipated their resolve."

"A little like the Vietnamese did to us later."

I never cease to be amazed by Sundae's insight. She catches onto things much quicker than two-thirds of my students. And from watching The War Channel her chronology was definitely improving. "Yes," I said. "In fact, General Cornwallis, who headquartered in the Carolina city of Charlotte, was harassed so badly by the local people that he finally had to leave town and find a new place to live. When he left, someone asked him to describe Charlotte, and do you know what he said?"

Sundae's eyes were wide. She liked stories. "No. What?"

"He said Charlotte was like a nest of hornets."

Sundae sat back in surprise. "But. . .but that's the name of the basketball team from Charlotte, isn't it?"

"Yep. That's where they got their name. Either that or the owners just lucked out."

"So they left us hornets alone after that."

"No, not exactly. In 1812 we got into another war with them, and they almost took us back over. They attacked and captured our capital at Washington."

"No."

"Yes. President Madison was about to sit down to eat in the White House when he was told he'd better get out, so he ran through the back door and hid in the woods behind the mansion while the English came in and sat down and. . .can you guess what?"

"They ate his lunch."

"Yes. Then they set fire to the White House."

"Bloody arrogant."

"You said it."

"But wait a minute," Sundae said. "On The War Channel they said that during The Great War and World War II we came in and helped save England's skin. Can that be true?"

"Yes, that's true. And we have been on their side ever since."

"Whatever for? Didn't they treat us like kittens? Didn't they eat our president's lunch and even set fire to his house?"

"Yes, they did all those things."

"Then how did we get to be buddies?"

"People don't have very long memories."

"You're right. Humans don't. You could learn a lot from cats. When we have an enemy we don't forget. Once an enemy, always an enemy."

"Some people say we got back together because we speak the same language."

"You're buddies because you both speak English?"

"That's what they say."

"That doesn't make any sense. I can speak Alley Cat, but I don't go to war to save every other cat that speaks it. That would go against my own self-interest. If the English treated us so badly, we should never forget it. We should never go to war for them. I agree with that skinny speaker tonight, the one whose Adam's Apple bobbed up and down when he talked. It should be "AMERICA FIRST.""

"Sundae," I said. "I'm not going to take you to anymore patriotic speeches. You're beginning to sound like a chauvinist."

She turned her head to the side and looked at me through narrowed eyes. "James, I don't know what that means, but I don't like the sound of it. Is it some kind of pig?"

Just then a shrill whistle penetrated our quiet home, and a shell exploded in the air just outside on the street. It was not part of the fireworks display. It was set off my some kid who had illegally imported it from Tennessee. It must have been his only one—or his parents put an end to his fun quickly—because it was the last of the night. But by the time the sound had died away Sundae was in my lap, her head buried under my arm. She stayed that way for a long time. I petted her and gave her reassurances. At last she came out and sat in my lap, facing me, looking slightly embarrassed."I really hate that," she muttered.

"Chauvinists can't be afraid of gunfire," I teased her as I patted her head.

"I'm not a chauvinist, whatever that is," she moaned. "I'm a pacifist. I'm a negotiator. I wouldn't have fought against the English, or for them. I would have talked them out of their long underwear."

I thought about that for a moment, and then I laughed. Sundae finally broke down and laughed with me. It was really funny. But then my town is quiet in the summer.

Sundae is my cat.

LABOR DAY

The rest of the summer passed uneventfully. I made a couple of trips out of town, but I was gone only overnight each time, so I left Sundae to enjoy some privacy. She has come to savor my little absences. She gets even more sleep than usual, I leave her plenty of food and water so that she's not hungry or thirsty, and she is alone long enough that she seems genuinely glad to see me again when I return.

The students returned to campus in late August, and Sundae and I live close enough to one row of dormitories for us to hear them, especially at night, when road traffic slows but students apparently do not. Sundae and I discussed this yearly immigration to our otherwise quiet little village and my minor role as one of the teachers of these temporary citizens who never sleep.

She failed to understand how someone eighteen years old would need to study anymore. She said cats learned most of what they need to know in life from their mothers during the first three weeks of life and that what they didn't know by then they can learn by watching television. Kids should be able to do the same. I wondered secretly whether she might be right, but I didn't admit it. When I agree with her too much she begins to act superior to me.

Classes began on the last Monday of August, and I was gone all day each day that week. Then came the weekend, and I was at home for two days, and the third day was Labor Day, and once again I was at home. Sundae noticed.

"I thought school was up and going," she said to me as I ate a late breakfast.

"It is. We've put in a week now."

"Then shouldn't you be gone already? Every morning last

92

week you were out of here by half past eight."

I realized that I was interfering with Sundae's television schedule. She was probably dying to see Oprah or Jerry or The War Channel, her three favorites, but she never turns the set on when I'm at home; and there I sat, drinking coffee on a work day.

"No classes this fine Monday, Sundae," I smiled, enjoying my little word play. "Because it's Labor Day."

"Labor Day?" she yawned. "Then why aren't you. . .laboring?"

I laughed, but Sundae didn't. She was perfectly serious. This was like so many things human: it made no sense to her. And when something doesn't make sense to her, it isn't funny.

"That's what we don't have to do on Labor Day. Laboring people get the day off."

"So on Labor Day no one labors."

"Not if you are a member of a union."

"A union of what? Marriage? You're not a member of that union."

"No. But we teachers have a union. I pay my dues. We negotiated for the day off, and we got it. Plus, most of the janitors and food services people are union, and without them the college just about shuts down."

"A union, then, is something that gets you off work."

I laughed again. "That, and it gets you better work, at a better wage, and better working conditions. It's supposed to do all those things for you anyway."

"So unions have to do with work."

"Yep. Mostly physical work. A union is a collection, a brotherhood or sisterhood, of workers. A union is for blue collar people. White collar people make so much money they don't need unions. In fact, they wish no one had them."

Sundae's eyes narrowed, and she crouched down on the floor

in front of me, then whipped her tail around and wrapped it about her back side. This was her way of getting comfortable so that she could listen carefully. It flattered me to know that she was willing to learn from me. This subject obviously interested her.

"Blue collar? White collar? What's all this collar stuff? Is it like my collar?" Sundae was sporting a new rhinestone collar which I had brought her for what we both had agreed would be her birthday. We chose August 1. It was as good as any day. Neither she nor I knew what her real birthday was. We weren't even sure of the year. Personally, I think she shaves a year or two off her age.

"Not quite like cat collars," I told her. "It refers to the colors of shirts that different kind of people wear to work. Professional people, the kind with college degrees, the kind who sit behind desks all day, don't get dirty when they work, so they have traditionally worn white shirts. They don't always, of course, because at times the rich folks wear stripes or plaids if they're in style, and white collar people are always in style, but we still use that term "white collar" to represent people who don't work with their hands, who don't get dirty."

"And people who do get dirty wear blue shirts?"

"Not always, but once they probably did. Blue doesn't show dirt. A lot of factories used to require their workers to wear uniforms, and they were often blue. Anyway, 'blue collar' is the term for someone who works with his hands. And they are the ones who need unions."

"Let me get this straight," Sundae said. "Anyone who works at manual labor is a blue collar person, is that right?"

"Right. Even when they don't wear blue. For example, the women who work in beauty shops, you know, fix people's hair and nails, they are often called pink collar workers because they so often wear pink smocks, but they are still blue collar."

Sundae sniffed in frustration. "So sometimes striped is white and pink is blue."

"Yes. And sometimes white is blue. You notice I often wear white shirts. I have a college degree. I work behind a desk much of the day, or behind a podium. I generally don't get dirty when I work, but I'm still, in my heart, blue collar."

"So you think of yourself as blue collar. But you sometimes wear a white collar. You also wear every other color of shirt. With every color of tie and coat. They don't always match."

"I thought cats were color blind."

"You are, that's for sure."

I felt hurt. It was a shock to learn that my cat noticed how badly I dress. I wondered whether my students noticed and commented on my bad taste in clothing. Probably not, I guessed, because most of them looked like refugees from The Great Depression themselves.

"Back to the subject, Sundae," I said peavishly, "I am technically white collar."

"Then why are you in a union?"

"Because I don't make much money."

"You're white collar, but you're poor. Strange."

"I guess we teachers should create a new category for ourselves," I said. "Maybe we should be called 'tattered white collar'."

"What?"

"You know, we wear white shirts, but the collars on them are old and frayed. Tattered." Sundae just stared at me. "Anyway, I plan to enjoy my Labor Day by not laboring."

"Humans don't like to work, do they?"

"No."

"Then why do you do it so much?"

"Some say we work hard because we hate work, we're trying to kill work. Then too, there's survival. We have to eat. That's why our unions fight to get and keep our jobs for us. So that we can work—and get days off work."

"If you didn't work, you wouldn't eat?"

"That's right. And neither would you."

That hit home. Sundae thought about it for a long time, the end of her tail flipping around above her head. "Will we eat tomorrow?" she said finally.

"Of course. Why?"

"You're not working today."

"I get paid anyway. See, that's the good part about being in a union. The union got me the day off—-with pay. I get to rest from my labors, but I also get to eat. Without unions that wouldn't be possible. Before unions. . ."

"Before unions? Then there was a time when they didn't exist?"

"That's right. Not too long ago. Then a man had to work every day, sometimes all day and all night, and if he didn't, he didn't eat. And sometimes the boss would just tell him not to come back to work, and he starved. Or sometimes he got hurt working, and the boss would just let him go, and he would starve."

"You mean, the boss would use him to work, and then when he wasn't useful, he would just kind of. . .throw him away."

"That's right."

"Like an empty cat food box?"

"Yep. Just like that."

"How ugly."

"Yes. And that's why working people got together and formed unions. It was self defense. Otherwise, they would starve."

"It's a brutal world out there, isn't it, James?"

"It sure is."

"Man-eat-man."

"You might say that."

"Tell me more. I bet it wasn't easy."

"Starting unions? No, it wasn't. There was a lot of violence. People got hurt, people got killed. The rich people were against unions. Most people in power, even presidents of the United States, opposed them. Working men would try to get organized, and the police and hired thugs would break them up. Sometimes they broke their heads, sometimes they killed them."

"Why?"

"So the rich could get richer."

"I thought humans were supposed to be. . .humane."

"Think again."

"I've always had my doubts about people."

"Me too," I admitted.

"So," Sundae said, giving me the cue to tell her more, "it was the whites against the blues."

"Yes. And the blues were at a definite disadvantage. Governmental officials were against them. They often moved around a lot, just to find work, and they weren't in one place long enough to help organize the unions. And in the early days many of the people who worked in factories were foreign born. . ."

"Foreign born? Why is that a disadvantage?"

"The rich could say they weren't good Americans."

"But. . .didn't the great, great grands of the rich come from someplace else too? Weren't they foreign born too?"

"Oh yes. But after they were here several generations they came to feel that they were the real Americans and the recently arrived were not."

"You humans!" Sundae sniffed. "You could learn something from us cats. We've been in this country as long as you've been here, and we don't feel like we're any better Americans than a cat who just arrived."

"What about the way you fuss with that mangy thing that comes up on the back porch?"

"We fuss. I don't tell him he doesn't belong in America, just not on my back porch. I don't want him to starve. He can form a union and demand better cat food if he wants to. You'd better believe I wouldn't oppose him."

"Good for you. So are you white collar or blue collar?"

She blinked slowly. "Rhinestone," she said. It was a joke. I knew it was, and I thought it was clever, but I forced myself not to laugh. After all, she wouldn't laugh at mine. She waited for a response but gave up on it. "So anyway, you blue collars, blue collars if only in spirit, like you, finally got your unions."

"After a lot of people were beaten up—and we finally got a President of the United States who favored unions, one who was on our side."

"Who was that?"

"Franklin Delano Roosevelt."

I must have said the name with some emotion. FDR is my favorite president. Sundae recognized the tone of my voice.

"Franklin Delano Roosevelt," she repeated the name with the same emphasis I had given it. "You really like him, don't you?" she said.

"I really do."

"Wait a minute," she said, her eyes glancing from one part of the ceiling to another. I could see the wheels turning in her head. "Roosevelt, Roosevelt. He's the one who led the Rough Riders up San Juan Hill. I saw him on The War Channel."

"That was his older cousin, Theodore. Franklin came later. He was president during the Depression and World War II."

"All right. Yes. Now I know. The one who had a dog named Fala."

"That's the one."

"If a man has to have a dog, it should be a Scottie."

"You approve of Fala, huh?"

"Not really. But Scotties, well, they look so stupid, no one takes them seriously. If I had to choose a kind of dog, you know, to show I have no species prejudice, a Scottie would be my dog of choice." She thought some more. "Franklin Roosevelt. He was the president with the really pretty wife."

"Eleanor Roosevelt? Pretty? Most people don't think so. My students look at her picture and ask why a good-looking man like FDR married a woman who looked like Eleanor."

"That just shows you how shallow they are. Mrs. Roosevelt helped people, didn't she? Poor people, black people, children? Pretty is as pretty does, isn't that true?"

"You've got a point," I smiled at her.

"I don't have much feeling for Franklin," Sundae said. But I guess if Eleanor chose him, he had to have been a good man. He was blue collar, I guess."

"Actually no, he was born rich. His was the whitest of white collars."

"Yet he was for the unions. Why? Didn't he know they would cost him money?"

"I guess he didn't care. Maybe if you always have money you don't worry about it so much. Maybe it's just the ones who recently got it who want so desperately to keep it from the ones who are trying to get it."

"Could be," Sundae said. "But I see Eleanor behind this someplace. I'd be willing to bet it was Eleanor who persuaded him to support the unions."

"I'll bet you would win the bet."

Sundae got up and crossed the room, heading to her bowl for a snack. "It's Monday," she said, turning to me at the door. "I guess you'll be watching your football tonight as usual."

She likes to scope me out about what television shows I plan to watch each night so she can decide whether to sit in my lap and watch with me or go to a quiet part of the house and sleep. Monday nights are usually times to snooze. She doesn't like football.

"Not tonight," I said. "It's Labor Day, remember? This is the night of the year when I watch the Miss America Contest."

"The what?"

"Miss America. You remember it from last year, don't you? You watched it with me. Pretty girls from all the states. . ."

"Walk across the stage and show off all they've got in front of a big audience."

"That's right. They wear bathing suits in one part of the contest."

"It's a meat market, James."

"Well, they wear evening dresses too."

"Still demeaning."

"Now, come on, Sundae." I had heard all the criticism. Feminists had been lambasting the Miss America Pageant for years. Was Sundae a radical feminist? "They also answer questions," I said defensively.

"Oh right," Sundae smirked. "What do you consider the world's most pressing unsolved problem?" she said in a deep voice, imitating the master of ceremonies, the easily forgettable young man in the tuxedo who had replaced the immortal Bert Parks. Then her voice went up three octaves, and she did a daffy falsetto: "Oh dear, world hunger, of course. And I just want to say that I plan to go into the jungles myself, after I complete my film career, and feed all the hungry little children personally."

"Sundae, please," I said. "It's not that bad."

"It's not that good either," she said. "I don't know how they pick a winner. They all say the same thing. And they all look just alike."

"They do not."

"A half size in the bust, a half shade in the blond hair, a half wit in the brain, that's about all that separates them."

I had to admit it. They did all look and talk pretty much the same. But this was one of the best television programs of the year, and I was not going to give it up. Even people who read books like I do, if they're men, like cheesecake. I took a deep breath. "Say what you will, I plan to be in front of the tube watching the boobs tonight. And no matter how critical you get, I plan to lust in my heart after the girls, and I plan to pick a favorite and cheer for her all the way through the program, and when she wins I plan to let out a whoop for her and dream of her all night long. So there."

Sundae looked disgusted, but she kept her silence. She went on through the door and out to the hallway, and I could hear her eating. She was chewing the dry cat food very slowly, the way she always does when she is either angry or deep in thought. I suspected it was both this time. Finally she came back in.

"Is Miss America always on Labor Day?" she asked me.

I suspected a trap. I knew she would want to get in the last word—-and let me know what she thought of my taste. "Yes," I said cautiously.

"Men got their heads broken, men died, Eleanor had to work on spoiled little rich boy Franklin, all so you could have labor unions, and the unions have worked all this time so you would get this day off, so you could sit here and watch a herd of vapid females walk across a stage in bathing suits. Have I got this all right?"

She can make me so mad. I sat there smoldering for the longest time, with Sundae looking up at me, waiting for an answer. But then a cool breeze, the first of the autumn, floated through the open window and touched my brow. I sighed. I can't stay mad at Sundae. I looked down at her and smiled. "You've pretty much got it right," I said.

"I thought so," she nodded. Then she trotted away to take her midmorning nap. She had beaten me again.

Sundae is my cat.

HALLOWEEN

Fall came early that year. By the third week in September the leaves were turning red and gold, and many mornings there was a trace of frost. By the middle of October trees were ablaze. Such autumns always make me remember the night in October so many years before when my daughter was born in the hospital on the hill.

I took her mother to the emergency entrance at 9:00 in the evening, expecting a baby by midnight, expecting to help deliver it. Instead, the admitting nurse told me to wait and I would be called when it was over—-and shut the door in my face. I stayed in the waiting room for the next three hours, until I was ready to burst with frustration, then went out to my car to listen to music and pass some time. The next thing I knew the sun was coming up, the windows were covered with frost, and when I went back into the hospital I was told that I had become the father of a baby girl. That's how I remember Octobers.

Near the end of the month, in fact the night of October 30, I decided to explain to Sundae about Halloween. There were two reasons for doing so. First, almost every day during that last week in October she had stood up from a mid-floor slumber, yawned and stretched, and bowed her back just like the stereotypical cats artists use on Halloween posters. Is it autumn that makes cats do that? I don't know. But as Halloween neared, she seemed to act more and more spooky. Second, I know how Sundae hates for people to come around our house, meter readers, garbage collectors, repairmen, even the paper girl, and I wanted to prepare her for all the visitors we would have that Friday night.

"Sundae," I said on Thursday after we had finished our dinner, "do you know what these are for?" I held up one of the seven sacks of candy I had bought that day.

"Cavities?" she mused.

"Well, yes, they do cause cavities, but I don't plan to eat any of them. No, I bought them for a special day tomorrow. Do you know what that is and why I bought candy for it?"

"You have a date with a new girlfriend."

"No. Why would you think that?"

"You usually start buying things like candy when you get a new girlfriend."

"Maybe I do, but it's usually a better grade than this stuff."

"Oh. Regardless of the grade of woman?"

I chose to ignore the dig. "I bought this to give to children."

"That's pretty cruel."

"No, it's not. They love it." The conversation wasn't going very well. Sundae was in one of her difficult moods. Usually I give up in face of such obstinance, but that night I went on. "No, I bought it to give to kids who come to the door tomorrow night, Trick-or-Treaters."

"You lost me."

"Tomorrow is Halloween, and tomorrow night, as the sun sets, children will be all over the neighborhood, knocking at doors, dressed in weird costumes, demanding that I give them a treat or they will play a trick on me."

Sundae looked off into space. "This all sounds familiar to me," she said. "Does this happen every year?"

"Yes. On October 31."

"Last year, at this time, they came around, didn't they?"

I had to think. For some reason I couldn't recall last Halloween. Then it hit me. I had been gone that night, out of town, and Sundae had been here alone. "Yes, they did," I said. "I was away. Did you see them?"

"Did I? It was the strangest sight of my whole life. The doorbell rang, and I peeped out through the shades of the porch window, and there stood these little kids, all dressed in strange costumes. One wore a sheet. One had on a suit that made him look like a skeleton. They just stood there for a time, and then they went away. The same thing must have happened twenty more times that night."

"Why didn't you ask me about it when I got back?"

"You didn't know I could talk then."

"Oh, that's right." I had learned about Sundae's gift at Christmas, and I suppose by that time, when we learned we could communicate, she had forgotten about the ghosts. "Anyway, that will happen again tomorrow night. Little kids will dress up like ghosts or goblins, and they will come up to the door and say, 'Trick or Treat,' and I'll give them candy because if I don't they have the right to play a trick on me, and they will go back to the street where their parents are waiting and then go on to the next house. At the end of the night, I won't have any candy left, and each of them will have a full sack. It's loads of fun for everyone, them and me."

"Oh boy," Sundae said with a smirk. "It's a real treat, huh?"

"Yep."

"What about the trick part? Last year you weren't here to give out treats, and I didn't see any tricks being played."

"No. No one plays tricks much anymore. Once they did, but it got out of hand. Some people played tricks without giving people a chance to give them treats. Sometimes the tricks were dangerous and sometimes destructive. So everyone agreed that Halloween should be just a night for little kids to get candy."

"So why say 'Trick or Treat'? Why not just say 'Treat!'?"

"Tradition."

"Oh yes," Sundae said. "Humans really like that stuff, don't they? You like to keep pretending things are the way they once were, even when you know they're not."

"You got it."

"Like Christmas."

"You remember."

Sundae sat there in front of me, mulling over what I had told her. "I guess what I don't understand is why you do this stuff in the first place. Do humans just have a mean streak, so that they need once a year to demand sweets from strangers or else they will do them harm?"

"Actually no. Halloween grew out of religion."

"Like Christmas."

"Kind of. See, October 31 is the night before All Saints Day, November 1. So it's called Holy Eve, the evening before All Holies Day. Somewhere it got corrupted down to be called Halloween. Can you hear the original words in it?"

"I hear them. But how did Saints get mixed up with tricks? Or treats for that matter?" Once more human tradition eluded her.

"Okay," I said, assuming my role as teacher, which of course I love. "It all got started with All Saints Day. November 1 was set aside as a day to remember all holy people of the past, so we could learn to imitate them and be good. Next came a tradition of preparing for this day, the evening before, so the night of October 31 grew in importance. Then came reports that on that night the Saints, all dead for years, came back and walked across the land, visiting us the living, and from that we got the notion that ghosts roamed the earth that night. At first these were all good ghosts who did nice things for people, but then somewhere people started blaming bad things that happened that night on the Saints-ghosts too."

"That doesn't make any sense."

"I know, but that's what happened. So pretty soon people hid out that night for fear some evil spirit might harm them; and of course mischievous or vengeful people took advantage of the general fear and the supernatural explanation and began playing tricks on people they hated or people they knew were superstitious. Then people started leaving gifts outside their doors to keep evil spirits from hurting them or their property. Then came kids, dressed up like ghosts and other evil spirits, kids everyone knew, who demand-ed treats or they would play tricks. Then gradually it became just treats, without tricks."

"So the tricks part is no longer with us."

"Oh, you'll hear about it now and then, but not often. We now call it vandalism, and just because it's Halloween, people can't get away with it."

"Good."

"In the old days, when my uncles were young, they still played tricks, and they've told me about some of them. A favorite one was to lead a farmer's cow up a ramp into the hayloft and leave her there. Cows will climb, but they won't descend, and the farmer would have a terrible time getting his cow down." I laughed at the thought of this, but Sundae didn't find it funny.

She sat looking at me for a long time, thinking, and then she surprised me. "James, I think I would like to do this Trick-or-Treat thing."

"You?"

"Yes. You could be my parent and stand out near the street, and I could dress up like a spook and go to doors and get treats."

I stared at her open-mouthed. I thought she was putting me on. I waited for her to flash her famous malicious grin, but she didn't. I decided to hazard an answer. "Sundae, you can't be serious. You're not a little kid. No one would give candy to a cat."

"So you're saying people would be prejudiced against me because of my species."

"Well yes, in a way. I mean, they might think it was cute, but they wouldn't understand that you can speak English and under-stand Halloween. They would just laugh."

"Let 'em try. I'll tell 'em where to go."

"No, you'd better not do that. Then they would know you can talk, and we would both be in trouble. It would be the end of your quiet life here in my house."

She thought about it for a moment. "I can see your point. How about this then? I dress up like a ghost, in one of those sheets, and scare them when they come up on our porch."

"Like a ghost? I'm afraid you wouldn't make a very convincing ghost. Certainly not wearing a sheet." Then I got an idea. "You could be a black cat."

"What? What do you mean?"

"Black cats are a part of Halloween. You see them in all the pictures. I know you're a calico, but I guess we could make you black."

I really meant this as a joke. I had no idea she would take to the idea, but she did. Her eyes grew wide.

"A black cat would scare people?"

"Yes. Black cats are considered bad luck."

"Why?"

"I have no idea, but people get scared if one crosses the road in front of them."

"Humans!" Sundae sniffed. "But I have to live among them, so I might as well use their superstitions against them. All right, James, how do I get black?"

I didn't actually know. I had never colored a cat before—or anything else for that matter, although I was considering darkening my beard if it kept getting grayer. "Would you sit still for me to spray you?" I asked, thinking she never would.

"If it helps me scare people, yes," she said. Then she added, "I will, if you will agree to dress like a ghost."

"What? Me? But I don't plan to leave the house."

"What difference does that make? Is there any rule that says the one giving out the treats can't dress up too? Maybe it would start a new human tradition."

I thought about that. Actually the man who lives across the street, who drives a public school bus, dresses up in costume for every holiday, to make a hit with the school kids he drives. I could dress up for Halloween. It would mean I got to see what Sundae looked like black. It might be worth it. "All right," I said. "I'll get a sheet and some spray."

The next day I went to the store and bought our equipment. I made sure the two colors of hair spray I bought, black for her and red for me, were non-toxic and didn't burn eyes and that it would come off with soap and water. I got home early, and Sundae and I began to get ready for our Halloween adventure.

She complained constantly as I sprayed and combed the black liquid into her fur. Fortunately she is a short haired cat, so the can had enough color in it to cover all her orange and white places. Finally I was finished and told her to look in the mirror. When she saw herself she jumped backward and hissed before she realized who she was; but then after she had walked around in front of the mirror and looked at herself from every side, she began to strut, proud of how frightening she would look to superstitious humans.

I cut a hole in the cheap sheet I had bought and put my head through it. Then I painted my face a deathly shade of white and sprayed the red dye into my hair. I looked in the mirror and understood Sundae's reaction to herself. I looked positively dead, positively gruesome. By the time the sun was setting I was ready.

Sundae and I took the candy, which filled three big bowls, to the front porch and sat down on the steps to wait. For a long time the street was quiet, with little traffic now that people were home from work. Then we began to hear voices at the far end of the street, and they grew louder as the Trick-or-Treaters got closer to us. Finally the first small clump of people arrived at the edge of my yard, and I saw a large man stop and signal for his three little tykes to go up to my house and collect their treats.

I heard Sundae chuckle in anticipation as the three little innocents made their way through the grass, bags open, ready for their harvest. As they got to the steps I stood up and Sundae rose beside me and stretched, then bowed her back. All three of the kids screamed, threw their sacks of candy into the air, and turned and ran back toward the man. I called to them, telling them not to be afraid, that I had goodies for them, but they kept running until they got to him and hid behind his legs. The next thing I knew I was in the middle of the yard, trying to calm their fears, and the man was raising a fist to warn me to stop. He was speaking hurriedly into a cellular phone. I heard him name my street.

I was still in the yard, too shocked to go back to the porch, when the police arrived. Sundae had completely disappeared, leaving me alone to explain our behavior. The tykes and their daddy stayed long enough to accuse me of all kinds of perversion, and then they left to continue their search for carbohydrates while I tried to talk my way out of being arrested. I remember only snatches of the conversation.

"Sir, we just don't approve of this kind. . ."

"I know, officer, but I didn't mean. . ."

"The kids are supposed to scare you, not you. . ."

"But I did it for my cat. . ."

"Your cat. . .? What cat. . .?"

It took me about an hour to talk them into letting me off. I had to promise that I would go inside, close my door, turn off my porch light, get out of the costume, and not answer my doorbell the rest of the night. They said they would keep an eye on me from now on. Insipidly, impotently, I thanked the Nazi Storm Troopers when they left.

As I climbed my front steps, Sundae came out from under the porch. I didn't speak to her.

I went inside, and she followed me. She came into the bathroom and watched as I washed off my white makeup and shampooed the red out of my hair. As I towelled off, I noticed that she was grinning at me, thoroughly enjoying my discomfort.

"Sort of backfired on you, didn't it?" she said.

"Backfired?" I said, rubbing my face. "On me? It was your

idea. I hope you're happy. I'm not."

"It just shows you how ridiculous some of your human traditions are," she said. "Trick-or-Treat indeed!" She looked at me carefully. "Funny, your hair is no longer red, but now your face is."

"And you're still black," I said. I decided to repay her for all my trouble. "You have a choice, Sundae, and you have to make it. I plan to enjoy it either way you decide to go."

"What?" she said, drawing back suspiciously.

"I can leave you black. . ."

"No," she said quickly.

"So you don't want to go through life being an Unlucky Cat."

"It's not that. I just want to be myself again."

"All right. Then you have another choice. You can either lick all the black off. . ."

"Can I do that? Should I?"

"Oh you can. But it'll probably kill you." I know, I know, it was a lie, but I was feeling mean right about then.

"Or—and this gives me great pleasure to anticipate—I can give you a bath.'.'"

"A bath? No." Sundae had never had a bath. She was deathly afraid of any more water than could be held in her bowl. She started to back away from me across the bathroom floor.

"Don't worry," I said. "I'm not gonna chase you. You have to decide. It's either stay black, die of lead poisoning, or come over here, surrender your will and wellbeing to me, and let me give you a bath."

That had to have been one of the most pleasant jobs of the entire autumn. Sundae submitted to her first bath. I used plenty of shampoo, and I gave her a second lathering, even though after the first one she was a calico once more. She hated it as much as I loved it. For a good half hour, as I scrubbed and rinsed her, knowing that she would itch for weeks in the dry autumn air, I chuckled as she swore at me and the world in general. I didn't know she knew such foul language. I have no idea where she learned it.

Sundae is my cat.

VETERANS DAY

I was angry with Sundae for a week about what happened to me on Halloween; and Sundae was angry with me for a week because of the bath I gave her. She spent most of the time scratching her itches, and I spent most of my time unable to scratch my itch.

Sundae and I had no conversations during that week. The only words we exchanged were monosyllabic, things like "move" and "bye" and "hi" and a few more things that didn't require any thought. Sundae and I were mad, hurt, insulted, and generally off-color.

Our silence prevented me from discussing with Sundae the next special date, November 11, Veterans Day, which that year came on a Tuesday, but which was commemorated on the Saturday before so that the traditional parade would have good attendance. That morning, as Sundae and I lounged in different parts of the house, we began to hear brass bands prepping. I live about halfway between the college and the town square, and it's not unusual for us to hear sounds equally well from each direction. We don't ordinarily hear music coming from town.

Sundae apparently listened to it for some time from the room where she was sulking before she finally broke our conversational fast by coming into the back bedroom where I was reading. Curiosity had finally killed the cat's pride.

"What's going on?" she said. She had a look of challenge in her eye, as if daring me to snub her when she was trying to resume our relationship.

"What? The music?"

"Yes, the music. Of course, the music. There's no football game today, is there?"

"Not here. The team is on the road. And besides, it's coming from the wrong direction. It's in town. They're gearing up for a parade. It's Veterans Day."

"Veterans? I thought we had a day for them, back in the spring. When you went out to visit your dad's grave and all."

"Well, that was for veterans, yes, but it was for those who are dead. The one today is for ones still living."

"If they're veterans, how can they still be alive? A veteran is someone who died in a war, isn't it?"

I've learned not to laugh when something Sundae says is ridiculous, unless of course she is being intentionally clever and wants me to laugh. "No," I said with as straight a face as I could manage, "a veteran is just someone who served in the armed forces. Some of them do die, but some don't, not in battle. They may die later, and then they are remembered along with the ones who died in battle; but the ones who make it through the war and are still living now, well, we give them this day, to tell them we appreciate them."

Sundae digested this information. "You say the music is for a parade?"

"Yep. It sounds like they're tuning up. Let me see." I turned a page in the newspaper I was reading and scanned the EVENTS column. "Yes. The parade is at 11:00."

"What do they do?"

"In the parade? Well, bands play, most of the local high schools march down the street playing patriotic music; and then the guys from each war go down the street, dressed in their old uniforms, and let people wave at them and give them a big cheer."

"Do they blow off cannons?"

Sundae looked worried. She hates loud sudden noises. The college has a cannon, without ammunition of course, and they fire it off every time the BIG RED scores on the field. Sundae literally hates football Saturdays. Once when I explained to her why the

ROTC boys fired off the cannon, she said she hoped our team never scored again.

"No, no cannons," I assured her. "The loudest noise you will hear is band music. I suspect the veterans would hate cannon fire as much as you do. They heard enough loud noises during their wars; and old men, even if they grow deaf, seem to lose tolerance for noise."

"I've noticed you don't play your music as loudly as you once did," Sundae grinned.

"I'm not old, Sundae," I said.

"You're getting there."

At least she was back to insulting me, which was a good sign. We sat looking at each other for a long second. I figured we were about to lapse into our silence again and take another three of four days to resume normal relations; but Sundae wasn't through questioning me.

"They wear their uniforms, you say."

"Yes, they dig out the old duds from moth balls and stretch their pants and coats over their expanded bottoms and bellies and try to look the way they did when they were twenty, or even when they were forty."

"So if I went to the parade I would be able to see some history. It would be like watching The War Channel all day and night, as they move from long ago to just yesterday."

"I guess so. If that kind of thing is interesting to you."

"Of course it is. How many wars will be represented? Will there be veterans from The Civil War? Or is that going back too far?"

"Too far. Way too far," I said. "Someone who fought in that war would be 150 years old by now. I think the last one died in the 1960s, and they weren't sure he was altogether authentic."

"Not authentic? How could be not be authentic?"

"Some doubted he was really in The Civil War. They thought he was lying about it. They said his physical condition proved that he couldn't be 120 years old."

"Would any from the Spanish-American War still be alive?"

Sundae's eyes were bright with excitement. She looked positively intrigued.

"Let's see," I said. "That was in 1898, nearly a hundred years ago, so a veteran from that war would have to be about 115. I guess it's possible, but probably not one here in our town. They would be few and far between, and our town's small size puts the odds against us. Even in the bigger places I can't see one of them able to go out in this damp cold to a parade. It would be inappropriate to survive battle, live past a hundred, and then die of a head cold."

"How about The Great War? The War to End All Wars? The war Mr. Wilson said would make the world Safe for Democracy? Will there be any from that one?"

"Well, the youngest ones in that war were probably born in 1902, since the minimum age would have been 16 when it ended in 1918. So they are over 90 now. Possibly."

"I want to watch," Sundae said suddenly.

"Watch what?"

"The parade. I want to see the veterans in their uniforms."

"Are you sure?"

"Yes. I've seen all the wars on television. Now I want to see the real thing. I want to see the old guys march. I want to see them get cheered."

"Sundae," I said, "why are you so interested in war?"

"It's the ultimate human folly. I never get tired of watching humans make fools of themselves. War goes against every logical principle, yet you keep on doing it, over and over. You even divide your history according to wars. All other species know better than to fight wars, and here you are, supposedly the brightest of all, and you do it continually. It's the most fascinating part of living under your rule during this period of time when you do rule."

"We won't always rule?"

"No. Once you didn't, and someday you won't."

I considered it, and I had to admit what Sundae said made sense. Our time in the driver's seat would inevitably have to end, just as once it had begun, and it would probably end because of war. We would deal our own selves the knockout blow.

"May I go?" Sundae said. "Will you take me?" It was about as close to a plea as Sundae ever came. She usually just told me what she wanted. This time she was almost begging. "I'll watch from the car window, and I won't say a word, and I'll behave myself."

She was so cute I couldn't say no to her. "All right," I said, "but you have to hurry. We only have fifteen minutes to get there. If we're late, we might miss a war or two."

Sundae hurried off to use her litter box and grab a quick mid-morning snack. I pulled on a heavy sweater. When we were ready I picked her up and took her to the car. We drove through the gathering crowds, mostly small family clumps, and I was lucky enough to find a parking spot along the town's one boulevard. I parked in the direction that allowed the passenger side of the car to be next to the street. Sundae was beside herself with anticipation.

At ten past eleven—these things always start late—we heard the first band approaching. It was obviously from a small high school because there were only twenty members, but they blew as hard and loudly as they could and made a good opening act. Two other bands followed, each one larger than the one before it, each one dressed in a more expensively tailored set of uniforms. Then came the first bunch of marching vets.

"Who are they?" Sundae asked me, her eyes were fixed on the marchers. There were twenty or so of them, and three were women.

"Desert Storm," I said. "See how young they are? These parades usually go in reverse chronological order. So these are from the most recent conflict. They fought in the Persian Gulf. Do you know about that one?"

"The one when Sadam Insane invaded Kuwait? Sure I do. The one where we said it was to protect democracy and freedom, but it was really to protect oil?"

"You're pretty perceptive, Sundae."

"It doesn't take a lot of brains to see through that one."

"I guess not."

"The good thing is that we won, whatever the reason. But we should've chased old Insane down and ended his career."

"Sundae, you really are a chauvinist."

"Why fight if you don't plan to win?"

There was another band, from another high school, and then an older group of uniformed marchers appeared. They all looked to be between 45 and 55. Most of them had beards. Some wore peace symbols on chains around their necks. There were several women among them, all dressed in nursing uniforms.

"Vietnam, right?" Sundae said.

"How did you guess?"

"You said we would go backward. They're older than the Gulf boys and girls. This was the war that caused so much trouble at home, wasn't it? The one you dodged."

"Yes."

I still can't look at Vietnam vets without feeling uncomfortable. I should have been among them, or I should have worked harder to keep them from going.

"Funny," Sundae mused. "They ended up looking like the people who protested the war. They look like anti-war hippies, don't they?"

It was true. Clean-cut soldiers had come home and grown beards, while bearded protesters had become clean-cut corporate executives.

"See why I enjoy the human comedy so much?" Sundae said, her eyes still glued to the passing marchers.

Next came a group, smaller in number than the Viet vets, in average age about 65, who walked with a rigid cadence, looking straight ahead. There was only one woman among them, a nurse. It occured to me as I watched them that the first two groups had looked out at the crowd, some waving, many smiling, all acknowledging to some degree the applause they got. The Gulf boys seemed to take the cheers for granted, the Viet vets seemed a bit surprised at it, and I saw tears in some of their eyes. These last men seemed unaware of having an audience. They had gone into war to do their duty. They were here today to do their duty. They would tolerate no criticism, and they wanted no acclaim. To put it succintly, they were humorless, colorless, thankless—and proud of it.

"Korea? Am I right?" Sundae said.

"You're right," I told her.

They were my dad's group. I guess it was foolish of me, but I looked closely at their faces, somehow hoping to see him—-or someone who looked like him. I didn't. I hoped he would still look as good as most of these men did, if he were alive. I hoped he would fight against the stoop in his shoulders the way they did. I hoped he would keep his grey hair neatly trimmed around the ears as they did. I hoped he would also walk with the kind of pride that needed no applause. They had returned to an America filled with economic opportunity. They had prospered. They had indulged themselves with good health care and expensive tailors and hair stylists. They had earned it and deserved it, and they didn't care what anybody thought about it.

Then they were gone, and after another band came a much smaller group, smaller in number and smaller in stature. These men were enjoying the parade more than any previous group. In contrast to Korea, these old guys were grinning and waving and laughing.

"World War II," Sundae said. She had stopped asking. She was now sure she knew. "The boys who beat Hitler."

"That's right," I said unnecessarily. "You notice how proud they are. Proud to be alive still.They're in their seventies now. Proud of what they did. They are the only vets who never had the least doubt that they were fighting for a just cause. And no one has ever questioned what they did. Must be nice."

"Must be." Sundae watched them. "Do they look little to you?"

"You noticed that too? Yes, they do."

I wondered if the years between 65 and 75 brought that much shrinkage in men. I had noticed how often the men of my youth looked smaller than I remembered them when I saw them again in later life. Was it because I had grown? Had they shrunk? Maybe these men were smaller than they used to be; or maybe men were just smaller back then than they are now. I notice also that every freshman class at college seems to get larger. When I was in college I was considered average in size, and now I'm small compared to the kids coming along. American diet has improved, no doubt about that. Diet in all the developed countries is better. These American "giants" from The Big War looked tiny.

Two more bands came by, the largest of the parade, and then nothing. I thought perhaps it was all over. Other people apparently thought so too because some started to move away from the curbs. Then we heard a loud, hooting, honking call. It was from a car, but it sounded almost like some animal from the forest. We all looked up the street, and coming at us was one of those cars made from a kit you order from a company in Tampa, Florida, newly created in someone's hobby shop but designed to look like something a movie star would have driven in the 1920s. A young fellow sat behind the wheel, and he was blowing the horn for all it was worth.

"What's this?" Sundae said.

"Look in the back seat," I told her.

We both looked at the two tiny men who sat there, huddled together against the autumn chill, wearing the olive green army issue of 1917, grinning timidly at the crowds on both sides of the street, occasionally raising a willow-thin arm in acknowledgement of the applause.

"Doughboys," Sundae said.

"The last of a breed," I said.

"They were told they had been chosen to bring in an era of eternal peace."

"President Wilson was the son of a Presbyterian minister," I said. "He used a lot of religious language. He was an idealist."

"He was a dreamer, and they fought for his dreams."

"Yes," I agreed.

Sundae watched them until they disappeared around a corner at the end of the street. . .and perhaps from history. Neither man might last another year. Then she got down from the window and sat beside me. I cranked the engine and slowly maneuvered us through the dispersing crowd. When we finally cleared the congestion and were on our way home, Sundae sighed deeply. "That's a lot of history we just saw."

"A lot, Sundae."

"Old men declare war, and young men fight. Old men live through wars, and young men die in them. Am I right?"

"I believe you're right."

"Do you think humans will ever learn, James? Think war will stop? Think it will ever be any different? Think there's any hope?"

"There's always hope."

"But it's not likely, is it?"

"No," I had to admit.

"No," Sundae said and nodded to herself for a long time. She lived in a human world, but she would never understand human nature.

Sundae is my cat.

THANKSGIVING—FINALLY

The year— my first full year with Sundae, the year in which we had held conversations about everything important to us, to mankind—was nearing an end. So was a romance.

Not Sundae's, mine. Sundae was neutered by the people who had her before I found her at the Humane Shelter, and she has never shown the least interest in love, not the romantic kind anyway. But since I was not neutered early in life—maybe I should have been— I keep searching for love, both romantic and companionary. My search has always been, and now continues to be, completely fruitless.

Since the summer I had been seeing a woman that I thought might be the one. She was close to my own age, and she was a great improvement over the ones I had found too young and brainless to keep my interest past a couple of dates. I really thought for a time that after all the barren years I might have found a companion. Then one day, out of the blue, she told me that a wealthy older man had offered to build her a house "on a lake" if she would marry him. It was obvious to her that I would never be more than a poorly paid classroom teacher, and she needed someone to take care of her financially as she grew older. She said, the way women so often do, "I hope we can still be friends." Right!

So the latter part of the year proved to be as depressing as the weather. I was glad to see the last Wednesday in November arrive and to watch the cavalcade of student cars, bumper to bumper, heading out toward the highway for the Thanksgiving weekend, the last before we would all have to buckle down for final exams.

I knew I needed to snap myself out of the doldrums. I needed to stop thinking about the fact I would probably die alone. I knew that cooking is a good recreation, and so I decided, even though no one was coming to visit, to cook a full Thanksgiving dinner for myself. Wednesday night I went to the grocery, bought the last turkey in the meat market, and filled up another bag with all the trimmings, or as they say in my town "the fixin's." I spent the evening, with Sundae sitting in the middle of the kitchen floor watching me, doing the million little chores that go with cooking Thanksgiving turkey; and before I went to bed at midnight I put the bird into the oven at a low temperature and let it baste all night. I woke several times, as Sundae jumped back to the foot of my bed from her many nighttime snacks, and each time the smell grew more inviting.

All I had for breakfast was coffee because I wanted to save plenty of room for the turkey. I turned on the television and took peeks around the corner from the kitchen at the various sports programs that got started a midmorning as I worked at potatoes, corn, rolls, cranberries. Sundae sat in a dining chair watching me through all my labors, a quizzical look on her face. As I was finishing it all up, as it was nearing completion, she finally spoke.

"I've never seen you work this hard, James, not in the kitchen anyway."

"I'm. . .inspired," I said.

"What's inspired you?"

"Well, it's Thanksgiving, and I feel grateful."

We talked for awhile about the history and meaning of Thanksgiving, about the Pilgrims and their first winter in New England and the good crop and how they had a meal, shared with the Native Americans, to thank God for their good fortune. Occasionally Sundae asked a question or added her own commentary, but mostly I did the talking, repeating to her the little lecture I had given my classes earlier in the week. I told her about how the Puritans had picked up the tradition and carried it on, even to the point of fining people who failed to observe the day, and how finally the last Thursday of November was set as the official day. I waxed eloquent about its significance. All the time I was speaking, though, I felt I was just a step away from bursting with sorrow. I might be inspired, but I was not happy.

"Thanksgiving. Yes, there's been a lot about it on television," Sundae finally said. "But what I've been seeing doesn't sound much like your Pilgrims and their celebration with the Indians. What I've been seeing is that you all stuff yourself with too much food and then fall asleep trying to watch football on television."

"I know. The ideal and the reality sometimes don't match up," I said.

"Why has it been so corrupted? Why do you do such foolish things?"

"Well, I guess the overeating goes back to the first feast, in a way, and maybe the Pilgrims played some games with the Indians, who knows?"

"It's confusing," Sundae said.

"It's one of those human things," I said.

"Obviously. Why do you people eat so much all at once? It's a lot better to eat a number of small snacks throughout the day—and night—than to fill up all at once."

"I know."

"And watching other people exercise? That doesn't make sense. You would be better off if you found other guys to play football with and did a game yourselves."

"Absolutely right," I said.

"You know that, but still you're gonna stuff yourself and watch college boys push each other all around the field on television."

"Yep."

She sniffed in frustration and moved away into the room where the television was playing to no one. I was close enough to the end of my preparations that I felt I could sit down for a while, so I followed her. I tried to get interested in the game that was on.

They had staggered the starting times so that a person could watch one game or another every hour of the day. This was two teams from a part of the country far from me, and I knew nothing about either one. They were big and slow and reminded me of two squads of wart hogs fighting over a loose turnip.

"You're really not into this game, are you James?" Sundae said.

I looked at her. She has the most uncanny way of reading my mind from the expressions on my face. "I guess not. Maybe things will be better when Florida State plays at 3:00." I'm a graduate of FSU, and although I have few fond memories of my struggle through school there, I still cheer for the Seminoles when they play football. I wonder how many men feel that way about their alma maters. It's almost as strong a tie as being born into a family. You may not be happy you were, you may have only miserable memories of growing up in that family, but you still feel kinship, and you still cheer for blood kin.

"Or maybe not," Sundae said.

"Maybe not," I admitted.

"All this work you're doing, it's because you're sad, isn't it?"

The little devil always knows. I had said nothing to her about the pretty blond woman preparing to move out to the lake with her rich husband, but she knew. I couldn't hide a thing from her. "Yes," I nodded.

And from nowhere came tears. I started crying, and I couldn't stop. I went on and on. I completely wet the front of my shirt and had to use my sleeves to sop up the overflow. Sundae made no move to comfort me. She seemed embarrassed by my show of emotion. But she sat with me, watching from another chair, waiting for me to get control of myself. It was only when I did that she said anything. "Feel better?"

"Some," I said.

"Crying, that's the only thing about human behavior I envy. I think we cats would be better off if we could do that. Of course, we would never do in front of anyone else."

"You lick yourself in odd place in front of other people," I said.

"What?" She looked genuinely puzzled. I suppose when she stuck her hind leg straight up into the air and went licking between her legs she had no idea it looked peculiar to humans.

"Never mind," I said.

"What's wrong," she said. "What's made you sad. You want to tell me about it?"

"I don't know," I said.

"I'm listening, as Frasier Crane says."

"Well, you know that lady? The one with the blond hair? She won't be coming to see me any more."

"No?"

"No."

"Are you surprised? You ran her off."

"I did? How?"

"You read poetry to her when you should have watched television with her. You bought her roses when you should have bought her a new car. You talked about taking her to England when you should have taken her to Las Vegas." She sat up and looked me in the eye. "You just don't understand human women, James."

"I guess not."

"Male cats and human women, they're equally difficult. A human woman should always have a male cat as a pet. They're so much alike. Equally unaware of anyone else in the world."

"Guess we're lucky to have found each other then, huh, Sundae?"

"You've just now figured that out?"

I laughed. It was my first good laugh for several weeks. I was still crying too, even while I laughed, and I must have sounded odd.

Sundae just watched me until I once again got control. I wiped my eyes and looked at her.

"You know what I feel like doing?" I said.

"No," she said suspiciously.

"I feel like giving this big Thanksgiving meal away."

"Give it away? To who?"

"To whom," I corrected her. I love doing that. Grammar is one of the few things I know better than Sundae, and it galls her to have me emend her English. But I didn't rub it in. "To the poor," I said. "If I knew where to find them."

"There's a homeless shelter," she said. "I saw on television about how if anyone wanted to bring food there today, they could."

"Where is it?"

Sundae told me the address. She looked coy. Her grammar might be faulty, but her knowledge of current events, and her memory for places, were exact.

It took me a while to find boxes that would hold all the food, tons of it, enough to have taken me a month to eat if I'd kept it; but before noon I had everything wrapped. Sundae didn't want to go with me, but she watched from the window as I carried it all to the car and drove away.

I left the food with a gracious lady who was preparing tables at the shelter and drove around town for a long time. I went by to look at the new cars at several lots, knowing I could never afford to buy one. If I could have afforded a car, I might have kept that pretty blond lady who now lived on the lake. I drove by the school where I work, happy I didn't have to teach yet strangely drawn to the salt mines. I stopped at the highest point in the town, under the city water tower, and looked out over my village. I didn't exactly say a prayer, but I was thankful. When I got home, Sundae met me at the door.

"Feel better?" she said.

"Some," I told her.

"You were gone a long time. Did you eat at the shelter?"

"No, I didn't. It never occured to me." I thought about it. "I guess it's best just to give food away without trying to eat any of it myself."

"Aren't you hungry?"

I wasn't. I hadn't eaten since the evening before, but my stomach hadn't complained. Then a thought hit me. "What I would like is a drink."

"A drink? Water?"

"I was thinking of something a little stronger. Let me look." I opened a cabinet door and squinted into the darkness. I saw a bottle of Bristol Creme. "It's Thanksgiving. I might as well try spirits."

Sundae eyed me coldly as I took down the bottle and poured myself a small glass of the syruppy concoction. I had bought this bottle in England, but I had hardly tasted it. Now was a good time. I took a sip. It was very sweet.

"How about me?"

"What? You? You want a drink, Sundae? I didn't know. . ."

"James, as I've said many times, there's a lot you don't know."

"All right then," I nodded. "I took down a wide mouthed glass, poured a small amount of the thick wine into it, and we went into my study. I put Sundae's glass down on the floor, and I sat in a chair with mine. "To us," I said as I raised my glass.

"Whatever," Sundae said.

We drank. First just a sip each. Then after we waited a few minutes to let the alcohol warm our tummies, we slowly finished it off. I may have refilled our glasses a couple of times. In half an hour I was relaxing in my chair and Sundae was collapsed, but still sitting up, in a corner.

"Good?" I asked her.

"Very good," she said.

"It's still Thanksgiving."

"You're not stuffed, and you're not watching football."

"I'm still single and living with my cat."

"It could be worse, James, it could be a lot worse."

"Yes," I had to admit. It could be a lot worse. Lots of things I didn't have, but I still had a lot to be thankful for.

I winked at Sundae, and she grinned.

Sundae is my cat.